A Tale of Two Tricksters

By Debbie Newcomb

To Kiran. Without you, this book never would have gotten published.

Long ago, back when magical creatures roamed the world as freely as humans do today, the djinns were to be avoided at all costs. They tended to live in the deserts and enjoyed tricking anyone they came across, including other djinns. They threw everything into chaos simply because they could. With unlimited power, no morals, and a love of trickery, there was nothing else to be expected. Then, King Solomon became able to trap these djinns in bottles. He placed a seal on each one that would not allow the djinn to escape. As punishment for their crimes, whenever one of these bottled djinns was found by a human, the djinn had to grant three wishes. However, no binding is perfect, and if the third wish was not used to put the djinn back into the bottle, then it could once again rampage across the land.

Our story begins with one such bottle, and the djinn inside. King Solomon had thrown this bottle into the ocean after trapping the djinn inside, and it was soon eaten by a fish, which was then eaten by a larger fish. After many years in the ocean, the bottle came up in a net, but when the fish were being moved, the bottle rolled away and no one noticed it. Through a series of forgetful people and animals, the djinn began her journey around the world, all without ever being released.

**

Leah snapped her mind back to the present as the cashier repeated her total. "Right," Leah said, handing over her credit card. It didn't really matter how much it was. None of it mattered. Woodenly, Leah took her food to her seat and willed herself to eat it. To stay in the present instead of flashing back to the doctor's office. Forcefully, Leah took a bite, determined to fuel her body. This body that couldn't support another body.

Eventually, Leah gave up trying to eat more and threw away what was left. There was a park across the road, and it was a good place to be alone. She hadn't told her husband yet. Not that they didn't know already, but it felt so certain hearing the doctor tell her. So unchangeable.

Her mind on autopilot, Leah walked one of her favorite paths to the pond. It was just chilly enough that no one else wanted to go this far into the park, and Leah sat down on a bench, grateful for the solitude. Then, without warning, it came over her again that she could never have a baby, and Leah started sobbing. It wasn't like she hadn't guessed something was wrong, but she hadn't thought she'd be infertile.

"Infertile," Leah thought. "I sound like a farmer talking about a tract of land." She looked down at the edge of the pond and noticed a bottle bobbing against the bank. Annoyed at the litter ruining her perfect spot, Leah stepped forward and pulled it out. She grabbed a few napkins from her purse to dry it off and wipe off some of the gunk. Part of her noticed it was pretty, but the rest wasn't paying attention. Leah began to roll the bottle between her hands.

"I wish," she said, then trailed off. "I wish I could birth a little girl, who would love me and who I could love." Leah sighed, knowing this could never happen. Her husband had suggested adoption already, and it was a good idea. It really was, but Leah had hoped to carry their own child first. Now she would never have the chance. She spent awhile longer, staring at the pond and rolling the bottle in her hands, enjoying the uneven texture of it. Finally, Leah stood up and put the bottle in her purse. She took out her phone and dialed her husband's number. She started walking back to her car.

"Hello," she replied. She listened, trying not to cry again. "Exactly," she replied. "I know, but it's still kind of a shock." She listened, and then smiled. "Thank you, honey. I'll be home soon, okay?" She smiled a little. "I love you too." Then she hung up and got in the car.

**

About three months after that day, Leah started to notice that her clothes were getting tight and she'd missed her period a few times. She didn't think much of it for a few more weeks until she noticed that she had missed her period yet again. Then, trying not to hope but being unable not to, Leah grabbed two pregnancy tests out of the cabinet and tested herself. It was the longest wait of her life, but both of them came up positive.

Leah couldn't contain herself. She ran out to the living room. "Mark!" she yelled, holding the two white sticks. "I'm pregnant!"

For a moment, Mark just started at her. Then, he began to smile as widely as she was. "That's great!" he said. He stood up and gave her a hug, which she fiercely returned. "What do we do?"

"I need to call my doctor. I'll have ultrasounds, and vitamins, and I get to enjoy being fat." Leah was grinning so widely her face hurt.

"Oh yes," Mark said, his smile dimming a little. "We'll need to make sure everything's okay."

Leah nodded, suddenly sober. Just because she was pregnant didn't mean she would stay that way. Or that she could safely be pregnant. "I'll call the doctor tomorrow," Leah said. "We'll go in and they'll tell us that everything is okay, and we'll have a beautiful baby girl."

"A girl?" Mark asked. "What do we do if it's a boy?"

Leah flushed. She hadn't realized she'd given the baby a gender already. "I just feel like it's a girl," she said and shrugged.

Mark laughed. "Well, either way. We'll have a beautiful baby." He kissed her. "And I'll cook for you tonight."

Leah laughed. "This is big news!" Mark had grown up with his mother cooking every meal and eventually, she had taught him how to cook. Mark rarely did these days because they could afford to go out to eat, and he didn't like doing all of the meal prep, but Leah thought his cooking tasted better than what they could order in a restaurant.

Mark laughed, rolling up his sleeves. "It's very big news. I have the feeling I'll be cooking a lot more now."

"We'll see what kind of cravings I get," Leah replied, giddy. "I've heard some pregnant women like pickles and ice cream."

Mark made a face. "Don't become one of them."

"I can't help it if I do," Leah said, teasing him.

"I can tell you I won't cook that for you," Mark said with a straight face.

Leah laughed. "Well, I'd better sit down. I don't want to overdo it, after all."

Mark shook his head and laughed. "We can't have that." He gave her a kiss, then he went into the kitchen to start working on dinner. Leah leaned back into the couch and smiled. At last!

**

The doctors couldn't explain it, but Leah had a normal, healthy pregnancy with a normal, healthy child at the end of it. Jennifer Marie was born a day before her due date, but at a good weight and with no problems.

"I told you it was a girl," Leah reminded Mark.

Mark laughed. "Yes, you did," he said.

Neither of them thought anything of the bottle Leah had brought home from the park and had ended up putting in their basement. Even if they had, they wouldn't have known the bottle was now empty.

Even from the beginning, it was clear that Jennifer preferred Leah over Mark. She would be quieter for Leah, burp better, and eat better. Eventually, they just accepted it and Leah ended up doing more of the hands-on parenting while Mark took care of other things. As they interacted with her, Mark spoke Mandarin to Jennifer while Leah spoke English. It was important to both of them that Jenn learn both languages.

As she grew up, Jennifer's strong personality became more pronounced. She used to speak Mandarin to Mark and English to Leah, but one day she switched. When both Leah and Mark replied in the language Jennifer had used without missing a beat, Jenn went back to the way it had been, clearly annoyed.

She loved hiding things in the house and then pretending like she hadn't. Her pranks started small, but gradually escalated. One day, Mark found himself yelling at her for balancing a bucket of water over a door she knew he was about to walk through. Jennifer was unrepentant, and Mark realized he had to send her to her room so he could calm down.

After Mark told Leah the story, she waited a few minutes, and then knocked on Jennifer's door.

"May I come in?" Leah asked.

"Just a minute," Jennifer said. Leah heard things being rearranged and was grateful Mark hadn't tried to come talk to their daughter instead. "Okay," Jennifer said.

Leah opened the door and shut it gently behind her. She sat down on the bed. "Jennifer, it's mean to play tricks like that."

"I know," Jennifer said. "Daddy told me."

"He was right," Leah replied.

Jennifer looked defiantly at the floor.

"I'm disappointed in you," Leah said after a moment.

Jennifer whipped around to look at her. "Why?" Jennifer sounded so hurt that it was hard for Leah not to react.

"Because you did a mean thing to someone who loves you, and you could have hurt him. Then you made it worse by not telling him you're sorry."

Jennifer struggled to say something for a moment, and then looked back down at the floor.

Leah shook her head. "I'd like you to stay in here and think about this until you can tell Daddy that you're sorry and mean it."

Jennifer said nothing.

After a moment, Leah got up and quietly closed the door behind her.

It took far longer than Leah thought it would, but Jennifer did come out of her room to tell Mark that she was sorry, and she did seem to mean it.

"I accept your apology," Mark said. "Please don't do that again."

Jennifer nodded gravely.

After that, her pranks moved more to the other kids at school, or the teachers. Leah got to know the principal of Jennifer's school really well. Leah was sure they didn't hear about all of the lies Jennifer told, but it was hard to know what all she told the other children. The teachers learned to double check anything Jenn told them. One of Jenn's favorite tricks was to suddenly start speaking Mandarin in class and pretend like she didn't understand English. This stopped when her third-grade teacher, who had spent a few years teaching English in China, replied back effortlessly in Mandarin. Jennifer stared at her teacher open-mouthed, and she never tried that trick again.

Leah was the most worried when they went to visit her brother, Daryl. He and his wife Starla lived on a farm. They had three kids, Hank, Donna, and Reina, and Starla was pregnant again. Hank was pretty unflappable, for a kid, but Jenn had played some nasty tricks on Donna and Reina. Leah had talked to her pretty strongly about it and, after awhile, they either stopped, or Leah stopped hearing about the pranks.

Despite the pranks, Leah and Mark tried to set up time with all three of them, or just a parent and Jenn to go do something. One of these trips took Leah and Jennifer to the museum. There was a new exhibit on the ancient Middle East, and Leah thought it would be educational. Jennifer thought it would be boring, but she was wrong. Jennifer was transfixed by all the pictures of what people used to look like and the relics archeologists had found. To her, it all looked so familiar, like that was where she should be. These were the people she should be tricking. The people in those pictures resonated with her more than her friends in school.
Leah crouched down and looked at her daughter. "What's wrong, sweetie?"

Jennifer hadn't realized she was crying. She shook her head and hugged her mom. Leah, confused, hugged her back. The people in the pictures were telling her she didn't belong, but Jennifer knew she did. She was supposed to be here with her mom. She told herself this fiercely, but it only helped a little. Although she managed to push that feeling to the back of her mind after they left the museum, Jennifer never really forgot it.

Around junior high school, Jenn, as she now called herself, cut down how often she played a trick on her classmates, and she began to make some friends that lasted more than a week. She still had some of these friends by high school, but Jenn could never shake that feeling from the museum that she didn't belong, even when she was in a group. When one of the girls chose to pass to her at soccer practice, or when one of the other flutists joked with her during rehearsal it made her feel better. For awhile, anyway.

It was almost worse for Jenn when they went out to Uncle Daryl's farm. Daryl and his wife, Starla, had a whole other level of communication. They had to be able to talk with just a look, since they ended up with five kids underfoot. Jenn had gotten to hold George and Perdita when they were babies. Both of them had seemed so tiny, yet so heavy. They completely trusted Jenn to keep holding them up and supporting their heads just like she was told. Part of Jenn wanted to mess it up, but most of her was too much in awe of these small humans. Everyone fit in so well in that house and Jenn both loved and hated it, but either way she was stuck with it. It seemed like since her parents weren't going to have any other kids, they wanted Jenn to get the experience of siblings by spending time with her cousins. Jenn wasn't sure what having a brother or sister was supposed to be like, but if it was like a visit to her cousins' house, she'd pass.

Around senior year, everyone was excited about which college they were going to. Jenn got accepted to the university in town, University of Eden Parkway, and that's where she chose to go. She was surprised by how many other people chose to go there as well. "I thought everyone else wanted to leave," she said to Julie, one of the clarinetists who was going to the local community college.

Julie shrugged. "Not everyone wants to, and not everyone can."

Jenn opened her mouth to say something about where Julie was going, but one of the percussionists picked that moment to start practicing his solo, and Jenn let it drop.

It seemed like it took forever and yet no time at all until the end of the summer when Jenn moved into her dorm room. There were so many new people who didn't know she would trick them. Jenn had a great freshman year. Leah had made Jenn see the importance of good grades well before this, so Jenn made the honor roll both semesters, but she had her fun as well. In one class, she managed to trick all of the students and the professor into adding a paper to the syllabus. He had been so confused that he couldn't find the assignment, but in the end, he had taken their papers and graded them anyway. Emma was in that class, and she knew Jenn had made the paper up, but both of them were easily able to write it, so they became friends. Chuck and Helen, who were also freshmen, also started hanging out with them, and the three of them were Jenn's friends throughout her first year, although they hardly ever believed what she said. Even when she tried to set up a love triangle, none of them believed her, although later Jenn wondered if Chuck and Helen had hooked up anyway.

After her first semester, Jenn had discovered the college of business. Her parents had said she should be a lawyer with how she bent the rules, but Jenn didn't want to argue on behalf of one person in court. Jenn decided on a major in General Management, and she really enjoyed most of the classes. It was fun to argue with a professor over a technicality and prove them wrong.

Eventually, Jenn's freshman year at college drew to a close and even the graduating seniors left. Campus town seemed even emptier this summer than it had in years before. Jenn started going out by herself a lot at night. Sometimes, she would hang out with friends from high school, but it was almost easier to be alone. One night, when she was in campus town looking for tumbleweeds, Jenn noticed the Velvet Tango Lounge. She hadn't gone there before because it was underground and didn't look like a good dancing bar. However, now that it was the summer, none of the bars were good for dancing because there was no one there to dance with. Jenn also wasn't wearing heels, because there was no one to impress, so she made her way easily down the narrow stairs to the door of the bar.

The bouncer asked for her ID and Jenn calmly handed over her fake. She hadn't been caught yet and, after a brief look, the bouncer handed it back to her.

Jenn hadn't been sure what to expect, but it was not what she saw. Despite its dingy appearance outside, the inside of the bar was elegant and made Jenn think twice about paying for her own drink. The lighting was dim, but Jenn could still see the paintings on the walls, real paintings not prints. The bar was in the middle of the room and it was the brightest thing, with gleaming wood, and mirrors behind the bottles in the middle. There was a jazz combo in the corner, playing smooth music. All in all, Jenn couldn't believe this bar survived in a campus town, but it was decently full for the summer.

She wandered to the bar and sat down. The bartender handed her a menu. "Let me know if you have any questions," he said, before walking away again.

Puzzled, Jenn opened the menu to find it was only for drinks, with a small blurb about the painting on the front of the menu. "What kind of place is this?" she wondered.

As she flipped through the menu, Jenn noticed a man sauntering over to her. She had played this game many times before, and Jenn tried not to smile. At least he was good looking. He had blond hair that fell away from his side part, a full beard that still seemed suave, and a dazzling smile. Jenn wondered what kind of tactic he'd use to pick her up.

"Need a little help with that menu?" he asked, sitting next to her. His voice was also smooth and sent a little thrill up Jenn's spine. He'd played this game before, too.

"Is this just for the drinks?" Jenn asked, playing herself down.

The man smiled. "It is. First time here?"

"Oh yes," Jenn said, making her eyes a little wider.

"I thought so," the man replied. "I'm Luke."

"Jenn," Jenn replied, shaking his hand. When they touched, something passed between them. It was strange, but small enough that Jenn could pretend she hadn't felt it. She didn't want anything from him except a free drink. Anything further and this would get too complicated.

"So, what's good here?" Jenn asked.

"There's no beating the view," Luke replied, looking at her.

Jenn managed to smile instead of rolling her eyes. "I meant to drink."

"Let me see," Luke said, turning a few pages of the menu and allowing their fingers to brush each other again. Jenn felt something again, but much less than the first time. It was hard to ignore it this time. "I prefer the gin fizz, but most of the women I've met here like the diamond fizz better."

"Diamonds are a girl's best friend," Jenn replied with a smile. Then she turned to the bartender. "Excuse me," she said. "Can I have a gin fizz, please?"

"Of course," the bartender said, nodding. "Anything for you, Luke?"

"No thanks," Luke replied.

"How often does he come here?" Jenn wondered.

"Adventurous, I see," Luke said to Jenn.

Jenn smiled. "I do try."

"Especially for someone underage. You could get in a lot of trouble for this."

Jenn froze. "I'm 22," she told him.

"I'm sure that's what your ID says. I'm sure it's even a good fake, but it is a fake."

"It's not. Can you leave me alone?" Jenn had never had someone reveal her this easily and it had her in fight or flight mode. And she was a terrible fighter.

"I thought you were enjoying the flirting," Luke replied with a smirk.

"Whatever. You're old enough to be my dad."

"Maybe so," Luke said, speculatively.

"So, are you leaving, or am I?" At this point, Jenn had no problem sticking Luke with the bill for her drink. That's what she was hoping to do anyway.

"That depends. Are you going to tell me what kind of magic you have?"

"What?" Jenn asked. "Are you still trying to flirt? Because this is the worst I've ever seen."

"I'm not, well, not any more than usual. But I would like you to answer my question. I take it personally when someone walks into my bar and they hide their magic from me."

"I don't know what you're talking about," Jenn replied, wondering if Luke owned this place. "How can I hide magic? It doesn't exist, and I don't have any."

Luke looked at her for a moment, and Jenn tried to calculate how long it would take her to run to the door. There was pepper spray in her purse, but she didn't want to use it.

After a moment, Jenn announced. "I'm just going to leave, if that's okay."

"It might not be. You've got vast stores of magic and things could go badly for you if you're not trained."

"Are you threatening me?" Jenn asked, grabbing her purse and debating again about the pepper spray.

"On the contrary, I'm trying to help you. Have you ever made anything happen? Anything that didn't make sense?"

"No," Jenn replied quickly. "There's no such thing as magic, and if there were, I think I would have noticed it." In her experience, people just got what they wished for, but in the worst way. That was just how the world worked. This guy was really starting to freak her out.

Luke gave her a measuring look. "Very well. If you don't have magic, then you don't. Pardon me." He stood up and walked away.

Once he had gotten far enough, Jenn turned around and headed for the door, not waiting for her drink. The bouncer stepped in front of her and held out a business card.

"What's this for?" Jenn asked, afraid he was going to stop her.

"It's from Luke," the bouncer said.

Even the bouncer knew this guy. "I really don't need to know how to get in touch with him," Jenn said. "Excuse me."

"Just take it," the bouncer said, moving in front of her.

Jenn sized him up. There was a reason he was a bouncer. She didn't stand a chance against him. Sighing, Jenn took the card from him and stuffed it in her purse. She was so busy leaving that she didn't notice the bouncer's face fading away to be replaced with Luke's, smirking at her back.

**

"Jenn, honey, are you awake?" Leah called up the stairs.

Jenn rolled over in bed and looked at the time. Right. They were going to Uncle Daryl's farm today. "I'm awake," Jenn yelled down. Slowly, she pulled herself out of bed. She had gone home right after that whole thing with Luke, but she hadn't been able to settle down enough to sleep for a long time. Something about him made her want to see him again, but then she remembered their conversation and never wanted to lay eyes on him. Why did this grown man seem to believe in magic? "If he was trying to prank me, he could have picked something more believable," Jenn thought, pulling on some clothes.

Jenn wandered down the stairs and into the kitchen. Her dad was reading the paper and blindly reaching for his toast on the other side. Jenn had added so many things to his food over the years that it was a wonder he still did things like this. Jenn wasn't awake enough to try anything this morning, though. Besides, that kind of prank had lost its charm for her. She pulled down a bowl and some cereal, splashed in some milk, and started eating.

"I didn't have time to bake anything," Leah fussed, putting a store-bought bunt cake into their picnic basket.

"You know, you don't have to bring them food," Jenn said around a mouthful of cereal.

"Of course we do. They've got seven people in their house, and farms don't make what they used to." Leah put some more fruit in the basket.

Jenn didn't reply. She knew her mom liked to worry about things. Jenn sometimes wondered what would happen if they'd had another child. Would Leah still worry the same amount about Jenn, or would it be less? Either way, there was no one else. Jenn was the miracle baby. Jenn finished shoveling breakfast in her mouth and ran to the bathroom to check her makeup before they left.

In the car, her parents listened to an audiobook that had something to do with the cutthroat world of business. Not literally cutthroat, or Jenn might have wanted to listen, even if they were halfway through. Instead, Jenn put in her headphones and listened to some of her music. It was a good day for guitar solos. While they drove, Jenn stared out the window, watching the cornfields go by so quickly, it was almost like they were flying. Idly, Jenn wondered what it would be like to fly. Then, she could feel it. The euphoria of being free of the ground, racing over sand dunes, the wind whipping in her face, all of it making her feel alive.

Jenn snapped back to herself. That had felt so real, but she'd never been to a desert, let alone flew over one. It had to have been a dream, but Jenn knew she hadn't been sleeping. It almost felt like a memory, but that didn't make any sense. Jenn turned up her music and tried to put it out of her mind. She shut her eyes to block out the corn whizzing past.

When that didn't work, she thought about her cousins. She hadn't seen them since Christmas. Hank was the oldest and he was in his second year of grad school, also at University of Eden Parkway. He was studying soil. Jenn supposed he was the sort who would have a garden, even in the heart of New York City. Next was Donna, who would be starting her senior year of undergrad in the fall. She had gone away for school and she didn't come home often since the plane tickets were fairly expensive. Privately, Jenn wondered how she could be graduating on time since she spent so much time gaming. Donna was a hardcore gamer, and the sort who liked to unlock everything. There had been several times that Jenn had steered her wrong and watched Donna's frustration slowly build until she had to call it quits.

Reina was next. She was going to be a senior in high school. Because she was a year and a half younger than Jenn, Jenn's parents had thought they would be great friends. Jenn didn't understand their logic. Reina was boy crazy and had been for years. Reina couldn't understand why it didn't drive Jenn crazy that she didn't have a boyfriend, and Jenn wasn't going to confess that sometimes it did. Reina was also very good at math and sometimes worried that was the reason she didn't have a boyfriend. Jenn wondered why Reina would want to date a guy who would care about that.

George was after her, heading into seventh grade in the fall. If you couldn't find him, all you had to do was look up. The boy was born to climb and it was hard to get him to come down sometimes. It made sense to Jenn. Their house was crammed with people, so being outside as much as possible was a good solution.

The youngest was Perdita. She was still in grade school and looked up to Jenn, trying to copy everything she did, especially if Perdita wasn't supposed to be doing it. Jenn had learned she had to be careful tricking Perdita. She was still young enough to cry at every little thing and it was no challenge to trick someone who believed everything you said. Besides, Leah was always disappointed in Jenn when Jenn got Perdita in trouble and that made Jenn uncomfortable.

With such diverse kids and a farm to run, Uncle Daryl and Aunt Starla surely had their work cut out for them. However, they tackled each day with an energy Jenn could only wonder at. On any day, you could find either of them driving the tractor or fixing it up, while the other one tried to keep the kids out of trouble. Hank helped with the farming as well, Jenn knew, but she wasn't sure how much help the rest of the kids were. None of them worked very much when Jenn and her parents came to visit.

Eventually, Jenn felt the car slowing for the turn off of the highway onto the local road. She was just glad the road they took after that had been paved in the last few years, so it was much less bumpy than when it was gravel. Jenn was so unsettled that she didn't try to make her dad think there was a deer or a dog about to run onto the road. She was a little old for tricks like that, anyway.

After not too much longer, they pulled into the driveway of Uncle Daryl's house. Almost immediately, Perdita ran out of the house and over to their car. Jenn got out to meet her.

"Hi!" Perdita yelled, wrapping her arms around Jenn.

"Hey, Perdita," Jenn said, ruffling Perdita's hair a bit, although there was a purple clip in Perdita's hair that Jenn had to watch out for. It bothered Reina when Perdita looked disheveled. Reina had given up on Donna finding true love, but she seemed to want to give Perdita those habits early. Whatever the reason, messing up Perdita's hair was a subtle way to annoy someone.

"Cheater!" George called. "You were watching for them at the door."

Perdita let go of Jenn to yell at her brother. "It's not my fault I got to them first," Perdita replied. "You could have if you weren't climbing a tree." She stuck her tongue out.

"I was trying to see them coming," George yelled back.

"Now, now," Leah said. "George, can you carry this basket inside for me?"

"Sure, Aunt Leah," George said, taking the picnic basket from her. "Did you bring us cake?"

Leah laughed. "We'll just have to see."

"I could look in it now, and then I'd know," George offered, walking to the house.

"Let's head in," Mark said next to Jenn. Jenn could tell he also had a hard time being closed in the house with this many people. Jenn could see why. The few times they'd made the flight to China to visit Mark's parents, their house had been quiet, small, and uncluttered. It was just about the opposite of Daryl and Starla's house.

Jenn nodded and shepherded Perdita in front of her as they headed in. When they got inside, Jenn was not surprised to see Donna playing a game on the TV. It was one Jenn didn't recognize, but it seemed to involve looting pyramids.

"Yes!" Donna said, as the screen showed that she had just gotten an Anubis head.

"Donna, say hello to our guests," Starla said, walking over to give Jenn a hug.

Donna turned toward Jenn and her parents. "Hey," Donna said. "Jenn, do you want to help me on this? The webpages always seem to load faster when you look for stuff."

Donna often played a game through once on her own and then a second time using a walkthrough on the internet to figure out where all of the treasures were. The reason the websites loaded more quickly for Jenn was because she made stuff up. Her crowning achievement had been convincing Donna that there was a treasure inside of a trap. Donna had gotten so frustrated, she had to turn her game off and go pace in the yard. It had been kind of nice to have the quiet after she left.

"Has anyone seen my purple hair clip?" Reina asked, walking into the living room.

"Reina, you're not going on your date until after they leave," Starla pointed out.

"I know, but I really want to use that one," Reina replied.

Starla shrugged and headed into the kitchen with Leah. Soon enough, Jenn heard the two moms laughing. She wondered what they talked about when it was just them. Maybe they had seen the hair clip in Perdita's hair too.

"You're going on a date?" Jenn asked, interested in spite of herself.

Reina nodded and blushed a little bit. "We're going to see a movie," she said.

"You should talk to him during the movie. Guys like to know you're interested," Jenn said.

"Really?" Reina asked. "I don't want to miss anything in the movie, though."

"You can always see it again with your friends," Jenn pointed out.

Reina thought about it, while Jenn debated about asking if this guy cared about her grades in math class. Then, Darryl walked into the living room and saw Jenn. As always, he gave her a bear hug and picked her up.

"You probably shouldn't be doing that anymore," Jenn said, trying not to let on how much he was crushing her. She noticed Reina walking away, still in search of her hair clip.

"It's no problem. You're light," Darryl replied.

"You don't have to remind me that I haven't grown since seventh grade," Jenn replied. It was true, but she also knew it would make Darryl feel bad and let her go.

Darryl put her down quickly and stepped back a pace. "College is really agreeing with you," he said. "I hope it's just as good for Reina."

"How many are on her list?" Jenn asked.

"About five," Darryl replied, "but University of Eden Parkway isn't on her list."

Jenn shrugged. "It's probably too close."

"Maybe for her," Darryl said.

Jenn couldn't understand why Darryl didn't want to get his kids out of the house, but there was a lot about him she didn't really understand.

Perdita came running over to Jenn. "You haven't seen our obstacle course yet!" she cried. Jenn noticed Perdita was no longer wearing the purple hair clip.

"You should check it out," Darryl said, "and take Reina and Donna with you. The more people, the more fun. Hank's still out looking at his test field, or I'd suggest you take him too."

Jenn knew he just wanted them to have another experience together, but she didn't mind this one. In high school, Jenn had taken up rock climbing, so an obstacle course sounded like fun.

Jenn, Perdita, Reina, and Donna trooped outside, with five harnesses for the course, and met George. It didn't take any convincing for him to come with them. As they walked to it, Perdita explained a little about it. "A tree fell down in a big storm we had in the spring. Dad said it was rotten on the inside, so it's just a good thing no one was under it when it fell. Instead of trying to move it, he smoothed it down and Mom built the rest of the course around it. It's really fun!"

Jenn was wondering how difficult this course was, when they came up to it. Jenn's cousins began stepping into their harnesses. Jenn looked over the course while stepping into hers, grateful she hadn't worn a dress. The tree that had fallen had been very tall. Jenn didn't blame Darryl for not wanting to move it. It would have taken a lot of time away from the fields if they'd tried. Luckily, it was in a windbreak of trees, and hadn't fallen outside of that, so it didn't take up any space in their field.

At the near end of the tree, was an upright web of cable. On the far end of the tree, was an angled wall of tires, leading up to a platform. From there, a line of monkey bars led even higher, and it ended in a zipline that brought you back to the beginning of the course. Jenn was pretty impressed by how sturdy everything looked, but if Starla had built it, she shouldn't be surprised by that.

While Jenn had been looking over the course, her cousins had started climbing up the cable web. Jenn followed behind them and was a little embarrassed at how slowly she was climbing. "Maybe I should go back to rock climbing and get those muscles back," Jenn thought, as she climbed down the other side of the web.

Her cousins all waited for her at the log. Once she got there, they formed a line down the log. What they had to do was have the person from the end of the line make their way up to the front of the line while everyone else was still standing on it, without falling off the log. Jenn was at the end of the line, so she was the first one to have to go down the line. There was a chancy moment when she was walking past Donna, but Jenn made it without falling off. Reina was the next one and, when she got to Jenn, Jenn wobbled until Reina fell off the log onto her butt. Reina laughed, stood up, and dusted herself off. Then she got back on the log to try again.

"I guess she's changing before her date," Jenn mused, letting Reina past her without difficulty this time.

Eventually, they all made it to the end of the log and onto the wall of tires. Again, Jenn was the last one and George was already starting on the monkey bars by the time Jenn made it to the platform. Jenn waited for the rest of her cousins to go ahead of her before she tried the monkey bars. Jenn grabbed onto the first one and let herself swing forward. That was a mistake. Her shoulders weren't used to taking her weight and it hurt. Jenn decided to finish this part as quickly as she could. Then they were at the top with the zip line. George clipped his harness onto one of the ropes at the top of the course, pushed off, and rocketed down the line, yelling all the way.

Reina went next, followed by Donna. Then it was just Jenn and Perdita. "I'm not sure I want to do this," Perdita said, grabbing Jenn's hand.

"Why not?" Jenn asked.

"Mom and Dad have always been here before, and this is really tall." Perdita looked down at the ground. "I wish I wasn't afraid of heights."

Jenn felt something in her hand, almost like getting shocked by static electricity, and Perdita started smiling. Perdita let go of Jenn's hand, clipped her harness onto the line, and shot down the zipline almost as fast as George had. Jenn waited until Perdita was clear, and then followed her. It was a pretty good course. Jenn wondered if they were going to do it again, but she saw Perdita sliding out of her harness and realized they wouldn't.

"George, I bet I can climb higher than you on that tree!" Perdita yelled.

"You're on!" George said, stepping out of his harness and handing it to Donna.

Perdita handed hers to Donna, and then raced toward the tree she'd pointed out. Donna and Reina took off their harnesses more sedately, and Jenn followed their example.

"We'd better make sure they don't hurt themselves," Reina said, following them.

"I've never seen Perdita like this," Donna said, following Reina.

"Like what?" Jenn asked, with the feeling she knew the answer.

"Usually she doesn't challenge George to climb things. He always wants to go higher than she does, and she gets frustrated that he always wins." Donna shifted the harnesses in her hand.

"Maybe the zipline got her excited," Jenn said. She refused to consider what Luke had said to her last night. This was perfectly explainable without magic and that shock Jenn had thought she felt was nothing. Maybe Perdita had a rough spot on her hand that had poked into Jenn at that moment. Jenn shook her head and looked at the tree in front of her to try to spot her cousins. Perdita was actually climbing faster than George.

"Perdita, slow down!" Reina yelled.

"No!" Perdita yelled. "I'm going to beat George this time!"

"She doesn't know what she's doing," Jenn thought, watching Perdita climb higher. It wouldn't be long until she made a misstep. Sure enough, Perdita grabbed a branch that was too weak, and it snapped. Perdita managed to catch herself on the branch just below it, but Reina and Donna both gasped.

"Perdita, you come down right now!" Reina snapped. She did a really good imitation of Starla's voice when Starla was mad. Jenn wondered how many times Reina had heard that.

"Only if George says I won!" Perdita yelled.

"You won!" George answered right away.

"What a pushover," Jenn thought.

Jenn, Reina, and Donna watched as the two climbed down the tree. There weren't any other mishaps. Then they walked back to the house.

Once they got inside, Donna stowed their harnesses while Perdita bragged to Starla in the kitchen.

"I climbed a tree faster than George!" she said, glowing.

"Yeah, but a branch broke in your hand," George told her, "so it wasn't a good climb."

"A branch broke?" Starla asked. "How high were you climbing, Perdita?"

Perdita apparently didn't hear the edge to Starla's question. "Really high!" Perdita answered with a big grin. "I don't think George has climbed that high before!"

"Yes, I have," George shot back.

Starla shook her head. "I'm disappointed in both of you. You know that you've got to be careful if you're going to climb a tree, and it does not sound like you were. I want both of you to go to your rooms until dinner time."

"But Mom," Perdita whined.

"No buts. Both of you march."

Perdita's lip quivered, but she walked away.

"I didn't even do anything," George protested.

"You know you shouldn't get in a contest with her about climbing a tree. It's not fair to her, and it's reckless. Go."

"Fine," George said, walking away as well.

Starla sighed and turned back to the cucumber she had been cutting. "Do they ever grow out of the reckless stage?"

Leah laughed, stirring the soup. "Probably. Not sure when that is, though."

"I'm not reckless," Jenn objected, picked up the sponge from the sink. She was frequently given chores here, and washing dishes was one of the easier ones, so Jenn tried to start that before she was assigned something else.

Leah gave her a look, and Jenn grinned at her.

"You're better about it than you used to be, but sometimes you still push people a little too far."

"I have no idea what you're talking about," Jenn managed with a straight face.

Starla laughed. "So, I'm guessing that major in business is going well."

"Yeah. It's General Management. Some of my professors were so unimaginative." Jenn mock sighed.

"I'm sure they've just never had a student like you," Starla teased.

"As long as you're studying hard, and they still give you the grade you earn," Leah replied, shaking her head.

"They can't fault me for reading the text and asking questions," Jenn answered.

Starla laughed. "I'm glad none of my kids toe the line like you. We've got enough to deal with around here as it is."

"I'm sure I have no idea what you mean," Jenn replied with a big grin.

"Of course you don't," Darryl joked, walking into the kitchen. "Do you have anything a hungry man can eat?"

Starla put her arm behind Jenn to keep her in place while Darryl walked behind both of them. "I wish you would stop saying that," Starla told him with a laugh. "Lunch will be ready soon."

Jenn had been hoping she wouldn't feel anything, but there was the same sensation between her arm and Starla's hand that she had felt between hers and Perdita's hand at the top of the course.

"Now, honey, you know I can't do --. Um. -- wouldn't be any fun," Darryl replied. He looked confused.

"What are you doing?" Starla asked. "Will you talk normally if I let you steal a few slices of cucumber?"

"Sure, -- would be nice," Darryl replied. He grabbed a small stack off the cutting board. "Excuse me."

Leah waited until he was gone before asking, "What's up with him?"

"I don't know," Starla replied. "He never did something like that growing up?"

Leah shook her head. "Not that I remember."

Jenn bent over the dishes, focusing on getting every last piece of food off of them. If she couldn't explain this to herself, she certainly didn't want to try to explain it to anyone else. Did Starla notice that jolt that passed between them? There was definitely something going on. Darryl wasn't voluntarily self-censoring the word "that" when he spoke. Jenn refused to think that slick bastard Luke might be right, but she wasn't sure what else to think. How dare he mess with her like this? She couldn't believe that guy knew more about her than she did. Had he done something to her last night at the bar? That made more sense than thinking she had magic and hadn't noticed her whole life.

Jenn had to get back at him, but she knew so little about him. All she knew about was that bar. Jenn rinsed off the knife she'd been cleaning and started on a pot. "I guess I'll have to ruin that for him," she thought. She probably couldn't get him kicked out, so she'd have to do something to the bar itself. "I could always burn it down," she thought idly. She scrubbed harder at the pot, remembering the guilt she'd felt when that branch broke in Perdita's hand. He had no business ruining her life. Maybe she wouldn't burn down the whole bar, but she'd start a fire big enough to mess it up. It wouldn't be the first time she'd had to get someone back for something they'd done to her. Satisfied, Jenn scrubbed the pot harder, getting all of the food off of it and down the garbage disposal.

**

The rest of the visit went well enough. Hank was really excited about the plants in his test field, so Jenn ended up tuning out for most of lunch. She saw her dad sending her conspiring looks of sympathy every so often. It seemed like they were the only two at the table who didn't know about farming. Eventually, they packed everything up and headed home.

On Monday, while her parents were at work, Jenn picked up a lighter with a nice, tall flame, but it wasn't until Tuesday night that she was able to go out. Jenn stood in her room, debating about what outfit to wear. Obviously, she needed sensible shoes in case this fire got out of control, but what else was she going to wear? There was no need to dress up for Luke, but part of Jenn wanted to wear something nicer than a t-shirt. Angrily, Jenn shoved down that part of herself, and pulled on a t-shirt that was a little too big for her, and a plain pair of shorts. She headed out the door before her parents could ask where she was going and drove to the Velvet Tango Lounge with a purpose.

At the door, the bouncer didn't ask for her ID. He just looked at her face for a moment, nodded, and let her in. "I guess he has a really good memory for faces," Jenn thought. She took a table next to the wall, away from the band. There was no reason to mess up their instruments just because she needed to get back at Luke.

A waiter came by and Jenn ordered a shot of vodka and a Sazerac. She'd never had a Sazerac before, but it sounded interesting. After the waiter walked away, Jenn pulled out her phone, and she was still on it when he came back with her drinks. Jenn thanked him. After he walked away again, she reached for the vodka and spilled it on the table. She clumsily wiped it up with some napkins, balled them up, and left them in a loose pile next to the wall. Then, looking at what she was doing, Jenn picked up her Sazerac and sipped it. It was stronger than she had been expecting, but it was still good. She fiddled with the cap on her lighter while she waited for Luke.

It took longer than she expected, but Luke came over to her table and sat down across from her. "It's a shame to spill a drink here," he said, indicating the mess.

"I know," Jenn said, and shrugged. "That's what I get for looking at my phone." She sipped her Sazerac.

"Can you get this lighter to work for me? I just bought it and I think it might be broken."

"Of course," Luke said. "I have a way with fire." When he reached across to take it, their fingers touched, and Jenn felt a different kind of electric sensation. Damn him. She couldn't tell if that was a different kind of magic or if it was an emotional spark.

Luke opened it up and clicked the lighter on easily and handed it back to Jenn. Jenn managed the bobble the hand-off and the lighter fell directly into the puddle of vodka. It didn't take very long for the vodka to catch on fire, and the napkins lit as well.

Involuntarily, Jenn jumped back with real fear in her eyes. Luke smirked at her. Then he reached into the fire and pulled the lighter out. When he clicked the lid shut, the fire went out.

"How did you do that?" Jenn demanded.

"I told you I have a way with fire," Luke mentioned. "You really should be careful with this." He handed it back to her again, and Jenn could feel the heat on it before she set it on the table. Luke looked at her. "So, that was your plan to ruin my life? Starting a fire in an underground bar?"

"Who said I was trying to ruin your life?" Jenn asked. "It was an accident."

Luke shrugged. "You made something happen, didn't you? You found your world view was wrong and it upset you. I'd say starting a fire was a bit of an overreaction, but my nephew would have done worse."

"Your nephew?" Jenn asked.

Luke shrugged. "He's a real hot head, not too smart. Anyway, that was your plan?"

"If it was intentional, we all could have gotten out before that got too extreme."

Luke nodded. "Probably, but you didn't answer my question. Did you make something happen that you couldn't explain?"

Jenn debated. If she wanted to get to him, she was going to have to get to know him better, but was it worth it? Should she just walk away and leave Luke to his secrets?

Jenn had rarely been able to quit when she was ahead. "Maybe," she temporized.

"And you came to me to find out more," Luke continued.

"If I did, what would you tell me?" Jenn asked. "Magic is real?"

He must have heard the scorn in her voice. "If you're not entirely in, then you're out. There's no half measures in magic."

Jenn stared at him.

Luke looked at her for a moment, nodded, and stood up. "Come back when you're sure."

"Wait!" Jenn said, trying to get her tone right. "What do you mean by magic?"

"You don't know what magic is?" Luke sat back down.

"I mean...do I get a wand and have to go to school for it?"

Luke laughed at her. "Not usually, no."

"It's not like I can just look this up on the internet," Jenn replied, a little stung.

"The internet has all of the answers. It's just some of them are more right than others," Luke replied with a smile.

"Maybe if you could show me something, it would be easier to believe in this," Jenn suggested.

"Show you something?" Luke asked. He considered for a moment. "I think I can do that. Come with me."

"Where?" Jenn asked immediately.

Luke smiled a toothy smile. "Still don't trust me, huh?"

Jenn decided not to answer that.

"You have my word that when I'm done showing you some real magic, which will be done well before the bar closes, you'll be able to leave in the same condition you entered this bar, and no one will try to stop you."

Luke knew how to phrase things very specifically, which was all the more reason to watch him. "All right," Jenn said, standing up.

Luke stood up, pushing his chair in, and led her to the wall opposite the entrance door. There was a door there that almost blended into the wall around it. Luke pulled out a small ring of keys from his pocket and picked out an old-school key. It almost looked like a prop key and not something that would unlock anything. Jenn watched as he put this key into the lock. Somehow, it unlocked the door, and Luke ushered Jenn inside.

The hallway beyond the door looked like a cave, but it was lined with doors. The sound of the door closing behind Jenn made her jump.

"Do I make you nervous?" Luke asked with a laugh.

"It's not often I follow strange men into a cave," Jenn replied caustically. "How is there a cave behind the bar?"

"There is and there isn't," Luke replied unhelpfully. He started walking down the hall, and Jenn followed him. Not too far down the hallway, Luke stopped in front of a door, fiddled with the keyhole, and pulled the door open.

Jenn was about to ask where he was taking her, when she saw what was behind the door. It was an enormous cave, with a pond against the far wall. Not too far from the pond was a patio set of a table and a few chairs. Closer to them was an empty bird perch, rising out of a narrow, tall cabinet. Jenn stepped inside the cave, and Luke walked in front of her, over to the perch, closing the door behind him. Jenn looked at the wall closest to her. Sticking out of the walls were small ledges with raised sides. They looked like beds.

Luke turned around to look at her. "You know you don't have to be afraid."

"I'm not afraid," Jenn said, her hand on the doorknob.

"I haven't even shown you real magic yet and you're going to leave," Luke pointed out.

"Why are there beds on the walls?" Jenn asked. "And why is the door locked? Is this a prison?"

Luke sighed. "It's a waystation. Not everyone who has magic fits in as well as you or I do. And even if they can pass, not everyone wants to."

Before Jenn could ask another question, a bird came soaring through the air. The light glinted off of it so brightly that Jenn had to look away. When she looked back, it had already landed. The bird was a beautiful cascade of rainbow colors, but its feathers glinted in the light the way feathers usually don't.

"This is the Achiyalabopa," Luke said, carefully running one finger along the bird's head. The bird opened one yellow eye and then closed it again.

"The what?" Jenn asked.

"Achiyalabopa," Luke repeated. "The Pueblo people talk about her. You're on the same continent and you don't know this?"

"Are those the people who built those houses?" Jenn asked, walking toward the strange bird. Slowly, Jenn reached out her hand and slid a finger on the top of the bird's head. Her feathers were warm, hard, and sharp. Jenn jerked her hand back. Sure enough, a cut was just beginning to well up blood on her finger.

"Let me help you with that," Luke said, producing a band aid from one of the drawers under the perch.

"I can do it myself," Jenn replied, being careful not to touch him when she took the band aid from him. She'd had enough of him. She looked back at the bird. "What do you do when Achiya... Achiyala... when she molts?" Jenn asked.

"We're all very careful," Luke replied, walking toward the pond.

Jenn decided not to push it. "A bird with metal feathers isn't really magic, you know," she told him instead, following at a distance.

"Achiyalabopa is one of those creatures who is magic, rather than using magic," Luke shared. He reached the edge of the pond. "Hey, Abe. I've got a student for you."

"The pond is a teacher?" Jenn asked dryly.

"Of course not. That would be silly."

A man with a long beard and long hair broke through the surface of the pond.

"He's a teacher," Luke told Jenn.

"Hello," Abe said. "Always nice to meet a new student."

"How did you get here?" Jenn asked, wondering if this pond could be an exit if she needed one.

"This goes far underground and all over the place, really," Abe said. "There's a lovely waterfall where we all sleep."

"You sleep in a waterfall?" Jenn asked, not sure how many more outlandish things she could take. She looked at Luke for confirmation, but he only grinned at her.

"Of course. It's very soothing. Now, what would you like me to teach you in? I'm an excellent scientist, although my astronomy could use a little work. I have studied all sorts of literature, but writing is so difficult for me. I always have to dictate, you see."

"Why do you have to dictate?" Jenn asked, trying to grab something in the torrent of words.

"It's pretty hard to write on paper in the water, and even if I write on something dry, my hair always manages to drip on it. I have to stay in the water, after all."

"Why do you have to stay in the water?" Jenn asked.

In answer, a fin rose up above the surface of the pond.

"You're a merman!" Jenn cried.

Abe looked a little hurt. "Why do they always think that? I'm an Abgal. We're protectors of the land, and teachers of the people. Nothing about singing sailors to their doom here. I'm afraid singing is one skill I'm still lacking in."

Jenn turned to Luke. "So, what did you do? Travel the world and grab up whatever creatures you could find?"

Luke shrugged a little. "Something like that. It's hard to live in some of the water in Mesopotamia anymore, and Achiyalobopa got tired of people trying to shoot her."

"And what do they do here?"

"Here? Some creatures recover, some simply stay on, until the day we can all return to our full glory." For a moment, Luke's face took on a different aspect. His blond hair became a dark, burning black, and his blue eyes burned like fire, his skin glowed, but his face became incredibly scarred. Then, as soon as it started, it stopped and Luke was a regular person again.

"Oh yes," Abe said, as if nothing had happened, "but for now it's been nice to protect a new land, and I have so many new students here. Even the most educated know about science and art, but not about the mysteries of life. The joy of travel and living off of the land."

"Living off the land?" Jenn asked, flashing back to her aunt and uncle's farm.

"Oh yes. It's much easier to do here than it is in the dessert. I do hope the others are teaching the Bedouins well without me. We all agreed that I was the best one to send, but sometimes I wonder."

Jenn wondered if Abe talked to himself when no one else was around. He probably talked to the bird, although maybe she responded to him.

"Our friend wanted to be shown something magical," Luke said.

"And you brought her here and not to a different room?" Abe asked with a wink.

Jenn did not like the implication that Luke should have brought her to his bedroom. She considered what would happen if she punched Abe in the face, but she couldn't be sure what he would do in response. Instead, she just glared at him.

"Yes, I brought her here," Luke said firmly. He sounded pretty annoyed. It would be better if Abe's comment hadn't annoyed Jenn as well, but at least it was something.

"Well then, what's your pleasure, miss?" Abe asked Jenn. "Dancing lights? Water people? Rabbit out of a hat?"

"I was wondering what it would be like to fly," Jenn said, remembering the vision she'd had on the way to Darryl's farm. It couldn't have been a memory.

"I can't help you with that," Abe said.

"I can," Luke replied. He turned to face Jenn and held out his hand. "Do you trust me?"

Jenn looked at his hand for a moment. He had sworn that no harm would come to her, and she had a feeling he kept his promises. To the letter, if not the spirit. Jenn set down her purse. Still dubious, Jenn put her hand in his. Luke pulled her closer and wrapped his other arm around her waist. "Be careful what you grab on to," Jenn warned him.

Luke laughed, and then they were off the ground. Jenn looked down at her feet, dangling in the air. It was amazing. It didn't even feel like Luke's arm was taking her weight. Jenn tried to push away from him, but he held onto her. "If I let you go, you'll fall," he warned her.

Jenn decided not to debate with him, as they were rising steadily higher. Once they got up close to the roof of the cavern, they started to ease forward. Then, they jerked forward and flashed around the cavern. Achiyalabopa left her perch and flew with them, weaving in and out, so close that Jenn could have touched her if she'd dared. It was amazing being up here, but Jenn wished she was doing it herself. That was crazy, though, she couldn't fly. Luke was the one keeping them up here. The thought bothered her, and she didn't bother to hide it.

"Everything all right?" Luke asked.

"Yes," Jenn lied. "That was great, but how do we get down?"

In answer, the ground rose up to meet them far too quickly. Without thinking, Jenn shut her eyes and prepared herself for impact. As she braced herself, she felt her feet land softly on the ground.

"Did you think I would let go?" Luke teased her.

"You can let me go now," Jenn said curtly, forcing her hand to open and let go of his. Her whole body had tensed up. Now she had two things to get back at him for.

"Magnificent!" Abe said. "A truly dizzying display from all of you. I haven't seen such artistry since the last abgal dance!"

"When was that?" Jenn asked, ignoring Luke.

"Last month," Abe replied. "Some of the abgals from other places have different dances and it was truly a wonder to be able to combine the styles of dance into one unique program."

"So, Luke brought other abgals here?" Jenn asked, shaking out her hand. She had grabbed onto Luke's hand in a death grip. She was surprised he hadn't said anything or apologized for scaring her. Then again, she probably shouldn't have been surprised about the last part. She noticed Luke wasn't standing next to her any more, but she was glad he left.

"Oh yes," Abe replied. "He's been around the world a few times, dear girl. Very experienced, that one."

Jenn couldn't tell if he was hinting at something else or not, but it didn't matter. There was no future for her and Luke together, so she didn't care about his past conquests.

"But," Abe continued like he hadn't paused, "Out of the abgals, I'm the one who speaks English the best. Got to keep up with the new trends, you know. I may be old school, but I'm not out of date."

Jenn couldn't help smiling at that. "You know your slang is out of date, right?"

Abe smiled. "It doesn't surprise me, but when one doesn't mingle much in society, it's hard to keep up with such fleeting phrases. Perhaps you can tell me about them sometime."

"Maybe," Jenn said. She wasn't sure she ever wanted to come back here because that would mean seeing Luke again, and after she left tonight she didn't think she wanted to do that. "Do you know where Luke went?"

"I would assume that he's getting a token of your experience tonight so you don't forget it."

"Forget it? I'm not likely to do that any time soon," Jenn replied, confused.

"I've seen people explain away stranger things," Abe told her. "That's one of the fascinating parts of psychology. If an event doesn't fit in a person's frame of existence, then they will twist and change their memory until the event fits with what they know."

"That seems counterproductive," Jenn replied.

"Indeed," Abe said, "but the human memory is unreliable anyway, so even if a person didn't change their memories, they still would have inaccurate ones."

"What about abgals?" Jenn challenged.

"We do our best to record what we have, but the water washes away our marks in the banks, even if they are stone, so ours is mostly an oral tradition."

"It would be hard for you to read a book, I guess," Jenn replied.

"Oh yes," Abe told her. "Achi only wants to turn the pages for me for so long, and I can't touch the book myself. If my skin gets too dry, it's a very bad thing for me."

"Achi?" Jenn asked.

"Oh yes. It's the nickname I gave Achiyalabopa and she seems to like it."

"So I could have been calling her Achi this whole time?" Jenn asked.

"Yes, but it was funny to hear you stumble on her name," Luke said from behind her.

Jenn turned around, ready to give him a piece of her mind.

"Here," Luke said, holding out a long, narrow block of wood to her.

"Thanks?" Jenn asked, taking it from him. As she looked at it, she could see the grip on one part, and how there was a slight break just past the grip.

"It's a knife made from one of Achi's feathers," Luke told her.

Jenn unsheathed the knife and looked at the blade. It was a blue feather with a slow fade to purple. There was a central tube and the outer edges were serrated. It looked just like other bird feathers Jenn had seen, except for the color and the fact that it was made of metal. It was beautiful.

"It's from the last time she molted," Luke continued.

"You sure know how to show a girl a good time," Jenn replied dryly, but her eyes didn't leave the knife for a few more seconds until she regretfully sheathed it. Jenn picked up her purse and put the knife inside.

"And now, if you'll allow me, I'll show you the way out," Luke said, offering his hand to Jenn.

Jenn was pretty sure the only way she would be leaving was if he escorted her. She wanted to look around without him and see what he was hiding. "Sure," she said, ignoring his hand and walking past him.

"Goodbye," Abe said. "I hope to see you again soon."

Jenn waved at him but didn't promise anything. They walked across the cave in silence and Luke opened the door for Jenn. He put his hand on the small of her back to guide her through, and Jenn felt a slight spark where the inside of his arm touched the back of her arm. She was getting really tired of being so aware every time they touched.

"I wish you would trust me," Luke told her.

"Which is one of the reasons I don't," Jenn said, walking into the hallway and stepping away from him.

Luke closed the door behind him and started walking down the hallway. Jenn stayed just a little too far away from him.

"So is this the reason it's your favorite bar?" Jenn asked.

"Is what the reason?" Luke asked in return.

"All of this back here," Jenn elaborated.

"Oh. No. I like the bar because of the drinks, the dim lighting, and the overall atmosphere. The rest of this came later."

"Hm," Jenn said. It didn't make sense. It would take a long time to carve all of this out of the rock. It couldn't have already been here when they built the bar. "Maybe it was magic," Jenn wondered. Then she pushed the thought down. She did fly with Luke, but she wasn't about to think magic could do everything. There had to be some limits to it.

Then, they made it to the door they'd come in through. Jenn opened it and walked through before Luke could touch her again. Luke pulled the door shut behind them and turned to face Jenn. "I hope to see you again soon," he said, with a smile that shouldn't have made Jenn's heart beat a little bit faster.

"Maybe," Jenn said. She turned around and resolutely walked away. She didn't look at the table she had burned, and she barely glanced at the bouncer on the way out.

**

The next morning, Jenn woke up remembering her flight with Luke. The sensation of flying had been so real, and so magical. However, in the bright light of day, it didn't seem like it could have happened. Jenn pulled out the knife Luke had given her and unsheathed it. Just like last night, it looked like a feather that that grown as metal, rather than whatever feathers were usually made out of. Jenn looked at it for a few minutes, trying to find some telling flaw or a maker's mark to show it had been made and not grown. Other than the two metal stakes in the handle to keep the feather in place, nothing else had been done to it. Which could just prove that Jenn didn't know what to look for. Sighing, Jenn sheathed the knife and slid it under her mattress. She didn't want to explain it to her parents.

They had told her that she would need to get an internship next summer, so Jenn was determined to enjoy her last summer of freedom. One of the best places to do that was at a nearby park. There were beautiful walking trails, and it was a great place to get out of the house and be alone. Jenn's parents were already at work, so they wouldn't have to know how much time Jenn was spending by herself. They wanted her to be involved and active like other kids her age. That just meant Jenn took pleasure in lying to them about how much time she spent with her friends. Of course, it worked the other way too. Sometimes, Jenn said she had gone out alone, when she'd really been with her friends, doing something they shouldn't be.

Jenn ate a quick breakfast and took her car out to the park. When she got there, Jenn was surprised to see some of her old high school classmates there as well.

"Hey, Jenn!" a broad-shouldered, sturdy boy called. Brad had been one of their best football players, but he broke the mold by also being one of the smartest kids in their school. He also wasn't as gullible as he used to be, sadly.

Jenn waved and headed over. Some of her best pranks came from moments like these.

"I'm telling you not to touch it," Trudy snapped. Jenn wondered if Trudy and Brad were still dating, or if the separation of college had finally broken them up. Trudy liked to be in charge and was generally obnoxious. Jenn was surprised anyone wanted to spend extended time with her.

"It's not radioactive," Bill replied quietly. Bill tended to fade into the woodwork if you weren't careful. He was still in high school, but usually was around wherever Brad was.

Jenn noticed there were some shears, a weedwhacker, and some other landscaping equipment near them. They couldn't be worked up over gardening tools, could they? Once she got closer, Jenn saw they were looking at one of Achi's feathers, glinting orange to red in the sunlight.

Jenn tried to control her shock, but she had not been expecting this. She knew if she had her knife here, it would match this feather exactly except for the coloring. It had to be real if another feather showed up here when Luke wasn't putting on a show for her. Jenn tried to shove all of this to the back of her mind and look calm but slightly puzzled. "What is it?" she asked.

"We're not sure," Trudy said. "Bill's kid brother found it earlier, so of course he called us over to look at it." Jenn looked at Trudy and guessed that she had been laying out and working on her tan. Jenn decided not to warn her about skin cancer, since Trudy wouldn't care anyway. Then Jenn looked at Bill. She would bet he called one of them over, and Trudy invited herself along.

"It doesn't look dangerous," Jenn said, reaching toward it. "I bet it's really flimsy."

"I'll decide that!" Trudy snapped, grabbing the feather before Jenn could. "Ow!" Trudy dropped it, blood dripping from her hand. "That's really sharp!"

"I've got a first aid kit in my car," Brad said, pulling Trudy away.

Jenn looked at the feather and back up at Bill. Carefully, she picked up the feather and set it in her purse. "It's a shame Trudy and Brad still seem to be glued at the hip. I heard Brad was looking for something different in his love life."

For a moment, Bill looked hopeful, but then he looked warry and shook his head. "He's stuck with her forever," Bill guessed. "Stupid."

Jenn agreed. "So, about this thing. We don't want the police all over this park, and I know I don't want to be questioned. Let's just pretend this never happened."

"Whatever," Bill said. "I'm not going to lie to the cops, but I won't call them either. It's just a stupid feather." He walked away, and Jenn remembered when Bill was younger and more gullible.

"I provide a public service," Jenn thought. "How else will my classmates be prepared for the real world where everyone lies?"

Brad and Trudy came back. Trudy's hand was covered in white gauze, which was starting to turn red. Jenn wasn't sure if that meant Brad had good first aid skills or bad ones.

"Where'd the thing go?" Trudy demanded. "It was right here."

"What thing?" Jenn asked. "You grabbed a pair of shears for some reason and cut yourself."

"No I didn't," Trudy contradicted her. "There was a metal feather. Right there."

"You've lost a lot of blood," Jenn said soothingly. "Maybe you should go to the hospital. You might need stitches."

"Stitches!?" Trudy yelled, shuddering. "I can't get stitches. It's so gross!"

"We probably should get you to a doctor," Brad said, giving Jenn a look. She knew he wasn't fooled, but he didn't care enough to pursue this. That meant Trudy was the only one Jenn could try to gaslight.

"Then let's go, before I bleed all over your car!" Trudy said. "What are the symptoms of blood loss?" she asked as they walked away.

It was always hard to tell if you'd tricked Trudy or not, because all she really thought about was herself. Either way, Jenn's mood was ruined. She wanted Luke to stay safely away from her regular life, and this feather showed how easily his world could move into hers. Muttering to herself, Jenn got back in her car and drove home.

When she got there, Jenn went straight to her room to get out the knife Luke had given her. Sure enough, the two feathers looked the same. It was real then. At least, the previous night had all been real, and that had to mean magic was real. At least in part. Jenn had cut herself on Achi's feathers, and seen where Abe's tail connected to his human torso. She had flown with Luke. But could she really do magic?

Jenn concentrated on turning the orange feather black. She thought about it with all her mind and pictured that it was so. The feather stayed the same color. "Either I don't have magic, or there's something else I need to do to use it," Jenn thought. For now, she wrapped the feather up in an old t-shirt and stuck it at the back of her closet. Her parents wouldn't find it, and Jenn could think about what she wanted to do with it.

Jenn apparently couldn't do magic on her own, but she could check into what Luke had told her. She pulled out her phone and did a search on Achiyalabopa. It took a few tries to get the spelling right, but then Jenn found it. The pictures weren't quite right, but they were close enough. There wasn't too much folklore out there about the achiyalabopa, except that it helped create the world. "That can't be right," Jenn thought. "There's no way Achi is that old. Besides, even if she were that old, a giant, shiny bird didn't create everything. The big bang did. Something that makes sense." Jenn set her phone down and stood up to pace.

Just because she believed in magic, however reluctantly, didn't mean she had to believe everything. She knew that lost people looking for answers were the easiest to manipulate. She did that all the time. So, Jenn took a moment to calm herself back down and go over what she knew about the world and the easiest way for Achi to fit into that. Achi could easily be magical and not be responsible for the creation of the world. That was just a story, while Achi was definitely real. Feeling a bit more settled, Jenn picked her phone back up.

She did a little more surfing and found that the Pueblo people had several clans, including the coyote clan. Looking up Coyote, Jenn found that he was a character in many of their folktales, and a trickster. He pulled some pretty good ones too.

Soon after that, Jenn came across Unktomi in the Lakota and Dakota Sioux tribes. He was also a trickster. In one of the stories, he saw a red cloud and convinced a few women to go try to pick the red plums that clearly had to be underneath it. While they were gone, he killed their babies, left their heads sticking out of the swaddling clothes, and cooked the rest. When the women came back, Unktomi served them the stew he had made and told them not to wake up their babies until after they were done eating. Once they realized what he had done, they chased him down, but he managed to slide away unharmed and live to trick someone else another day.

Part of Jenn admired Unktomi's trick. It was entirely needless, but it was clever beyond belief. Those women would feel the impact of that for a long time. Part of Jenn was horrified that he would kill babies and make their mothers eat them. "A different time, I guess," Jenn thought, still uneasy. "Still, they had to have known he was a trickster. There's so many other stories about him too!"

Shaking her head, Jenn locked her phone and headed to the kitchen to get some lunch. While she was microwaving last night's leftovers, Jenn considered what she knew. The Achiyalabopa seemed like a good bird in the stories, so that either meant that Luke was a good guy, or that Achi had been duped into believing he was. "Or that Achi doesn't want to be good anymore and is willing to go along with whatever plan Luke cooks up," Jenn thought, taking her food out of the microwave. All she really had were half-truths, and those were easy to twist and give someone something that was just true enough, while still being a lie.

Jenn sat down at the table and started eating. "What would Luke want to trick me about anyway?" she wondered. It could be the existence of magic, but that had seemed pretty real, what with the bird with metal feathers, the abgal with a tail, and flying around the cavern. Then again, that had all happened while Luke was there. Jenn needed to get back into that cave when he was gone. Then she could look in a few of those other doors as well. Maybe that would give her some answers about what he was up to. "But how am I going to get in there?" Jenn wondered, finishing her food. "I can't exactly pick the lock while the bar's open, and I don't think I can get in there after hours." Jenn rinsed her dishes and put them in the dishwasher.

Then it hit her. If Achi lost a feather in the park, then she had to be able to fly there. Maybe there was a way into those caves nearby. It would be hard to get into, since she didn't have a pair of wings, but she did still have her climbing equipment from high school. Even if the cave were up high with a long drop back inside, she should still be able to climb it. Jenn tried to remember what all she would need for climbing. Definitely a helmet, some rope, and a crap ton of carabiners. Jenn pulled up the internet on her phone and started typing. After not too much work, Jenn came up with a list. She was pretty sure she had most of this stuff, but she knew there were a least a few things she would need to buy.

All of her old climbing gear was in a tub in the attic. Of course, their attic was accessed by a pull-down door in the hallway. So, if Jenn wanted to get anything out of there surreptitiously, she would need to get it down now, while her parents were still at work. Jenn slid her phone into her pocket and got into the attic.

There was more stuff up here than she remembered, and the single light didn't go very far. Jenn didn't remember which tub her equipment was in, so she started rummaging through boxes. She found her parents' wedding album, and some of her old baby stuff before she found what she was looking for. The first thing she saw was her bright orange helmet. Jenn put it on and smacked the sides. It seemed to be in good condition, but she would have to paint it black before she could try a climb at night. Then she pulled out her quick draws, carabiners, harness, climbing shoes, and a few other odds and ends. The shoes had been bent into a weird shape, but Jenn was pretty sure they would flatten out after she wore them for a bit.

She still had her ropes, but they looked a little frayed and there was no way Jenn was going to trust her weight to those. She would need some belaying points, since she was probably going to be making this trail herself, and a belaying device, as well as some chalk to give her hands a better grip. With some mental calculations, Jenn figured it wouldn't be too much money to buy all of this. She would take the money out of an ATM first so her parents didn't know what she was spending the money on.

Jenn checked the time. She would need to move quickly to get all of this into her room before her mom came home. Jenn scooped up as much as she could and brought it down and into her room. She had to make two trips, and she was just pushing the attic door back into place, when she heard the garage door open. Jenn dusted herself off and dropped onto her bed, with her phone in her hand.

"I'm home!" Leah yelled.

"Hi, Mom!" Jenn yelled back.

There were a few seconds of silence while Jenn's mom stepped out of her shoes and put her purse down. Then Jenn heard her walking over toward her. Leah knocked on the open door.

"Hey," Jenn said, putting her phone down.

"What were you up to today?" Leah asked.

"Oh, saving the world," Jenn replied nonchalantly. "How about you?"

Leah laughed. "Oh, putting out fires, giving people things they should have had already. You know, my usual day." Leah worked at the big hospital in town, Lambert Hospital. She was in some sort of administrative role but from the stories, Jenn was pretty sure the hospital depended on Leah to keep running. She had asked and Leah had denied it, but that was Leah all over.

Leah said something like this almost every day, but Jenn could tell Leah enjoyed her job.

"So, what's for dinner?" Jenn asked, looking for takeout bags in her mom's hands.

"Typical," Leah said with a smile. "I got some chicken from the store, and I was thinking we could heat up some vegetables to go with it."

"Sounds good to me," Jenn replied. "I'll deal with the chicken."

"Great. Let me get changed and I'll meet you in the kitchen."

Jenn went into the kitchen and was a little disappointed at what she found in the grocery bags. "Mom, you didn't say the chicken was frozen." Jenn put a bit of whine in her voice.

"I know," Leah said. "I also didn't say it was rotisserie and ready to go. Sorry, dear. You've got to work for your food tonight."

Jenn stuck her tongue out but pulled out a pan and put it on the stove. She hated being beaten at her own game. At least she could look at her phone as she stirred the chicken in the pan. Every so often, she'd glance over to make sure it was all staying put.

Once the chicken was almost completely defrosted, Leah dumped half a bag of frozen broccoli in a bowl, put in a bit of water, and put the whole thing in the microwave.

"Taking the easy job," Jenn sassed her mom.

"Whenever I can," Leah replied. "It's been enough work raising you."

Jenn pretended to be offended, but she couldn't help but laugh. She knew it was true and it was pretty funny.

Just about the time everything was ready, Mark came home. "Smells great, ladies," he told them. "Let me just get changed, and I'll be ready to eat."

"Why doesn't Dad cook for us anymore?" Jenn asked, mostly to be a pain, but part of her did wonder.

"Well, the Asian store near us closed, so it's harder to get some of the ingredients, and he doesn't always have time." Jenn saw that Leah looked a little impatient with these excuses, but Jenn wasn't sure if she should push this or not. It was no fun upsetting her mother.

"And I'm not here to chop vegetables for him anyway," Jenn pointed out. That was the main thing she remembered about when her dad cooked for them. All of his dishes were from scratch and required quite a bit of prep work. They were delicious in the end, but Jenn wasn't always sure it was worth it.

Leah laughed. "That's true." She took the broccoli out of the microwave and put it on the table. Jenn followed behind her with the chicken. Just after they sat down, Mark came into the kitchen.

"What do you want to drink?" he asked them.

Leah asked for water and Jenn asked for pop. Mark brought in their drinks and a beer for himself.

"Tough day at work?" Leah asked.

"No, actually. Tom finally unbent enough to listen to my proposal."

"That's great!" Leah said.

Jenn tuned out. There was often a new idea her dad had to make his company better, but it was hard to get people to change, so he got frustrated when no one would listen to him. Jenn wondered why he didn't change jobs, but she supposed part of him liked the challenge.

"How was your day?" Mark asked Jenn.

"Oh. It was good," Jenn replied. "The internet is still there. I checked."

"You are getting an internship next summer," Mark stated.

"Yes," Leah agreed. "Next summer." She turned to Jenn. "You'll be working the rest of your life. Enjoy the freedom while you can."

"If you save enough, you can retire early," Mark pointed out.

Leah shook her head with a small smile. "Just like you're doing?"

Mark looked for words, and then shrugged. "I didn't work hard enough to make that happen, but I could have."

Jenn got impatient when her parents started talking about grownup stuff like that. She wouldn't have to worry about that for awhile yet. "I'm going to go see what my friends are up to tonight," she said.

"Okay, sweetie. Don't stay out too late." Leah smiled at Jenn.

"I promise to be back before you leave in the morning," Jenn replied.

"A few hours before that, please," Mark said, raising an eyebrow.

Jenn mock sighed and put her dishes in the dishwasher, then headed to her room. She wanted to try her lock picks against that lock in the Velvet Tango Lounge one of these days, but she would have to get into the bar when no one was in it. Otherwise someone would definitely see what she was doing. Jenn wandered to her room and decided to look up the bar hours on her computer. Then she could at least see when it would be possible to get in there. When she pulled up their Facebook page, she saw they would be closed for repairs tomorrow. The timing couldn't be better. Jenn smiled, and grabbed her purse. Years ago, she had modified two bobby pins to serve as her lock picks and they hadn't failed her yet. They were in her wallet, where she had left them. Jenn put them back and smiled.

    That took care of what she would do tomorrow, but what about tonight? Jenn pondered and realized she hadn't seen Julie in awhile. Jenn wondered if her classmate had forgotten to take everything Jenn said with a healthy dose of skepticism. There was only one way to find out. Jenn texted Julie, "You wanna see a movie?"

    Jenn didn't have to wait long for a reply. "Sure."

    They haggled about a movie for a bit before deciding. Jenn had just enough time to swing by the dollar store and get some candy before she had to get to the theater.

    Jenn headed to the door. "I'm going to see a movie," she told her parents as she walked by.

    "Bye, sweetie," Leah replied.

    "Don't stay out too late," Mark told her.

    "I'll be back before sunrise," Jenn teased. Then she was out the door.

**

    Jenn got to the theater a bit early, so she waited for Julie in the lobby. Then she waited some more. Eventually, Jenn had to go in the theater or risk missing the beginning of the movie. Decidedly annoyed, Jenn went in the theater and took a seat. This was the kind of thing she would have done a few years ago. Maybe Julie did remember how Jenn liked to play tricks. Jenn was just figuring out what she was going to do to pay her back, when someone walked into the theater. It turned out to be Julie, who quickly found Jenn and sat down.

"Sorry I'm late," Julie whispered. "My dad had to put in overtime and he was late bringing the car back."

"No worries," Jenn replied. Julie was too nice to think of a lie like that, so Jenn believed her.

It was a decent movie, but it bothered Jenn that right when the villain was about to win, he caved and turned off his doomsday device.

While the credits rolled, Jenn complained about this to Julie.

"But if he hadn't turned it off, he would have blown up the woman he loved," Julie argued.

Jenn snorted. "Love? He barely knew her. What a terrible reason to abandon such a complicated plan."

"Sometimes I forget how you see the world," Julie replied, shaking her head.

"What do you mean?" Jenn asked.

"You value winning more than you do people."

"Hey, it's a dog eat dog world," Jenn replied. Why bother to care about people who didn't care about you anyway?

They watched the credits roll.

"Do you think there's anything after them?" Jenn asked.

Julie shrugged. "I'm not sure, but if we don't stay and watch, we'll never know."

This wasn't quite true, but Jenn didn't have any other plans for the night. As it turned out, there was a scene at the end. The villain broke out of the maximum-security prison. "I'll be back, and this time no mercy!" he vowed.

The lights came on and Jenn and Julie stood up. "So, the subtitle of the sequel will be No Mercy," Jenn predicted.

Julie laughed. "Probably." They left the theater and stopped. "Okay, don't look now, but this hot guy is looking at you," Julie said.

Of course, Jenn turned to look. She shouldn't have been surprised that it was Luke. "You think he's hot?" she asked Julie, curious.

Julie shrugged. "I like guys a little older. Then they're finally grown up."

"This one isn't," Jenn replied.

"You know him?" Julie asked.

Jenn nodded.

"That's a little weird, then," Julie replied.

Jenn nodded again. They didn't have time for anything else because Luke stopped next to them. "Taking in a movie?" Jenn asked him sarcastically.

"Yes," Luke replied. "I didn't know you liked movies too. Who is your charming friend?"

"Luke, Julie, Julie, Luke," Jenn replied. Luke offered his hand, and Julie shook it. Jenn looked back at Luke. "Why are you following me?"

"Following you? I simply wanted to watch a movie," Luke replied, pretending to be hurt. "I'm a big fan of this sort of film, but I do wish the villain hadn't thrown everything away at the end. It's rather out of character for him."

"That's what Jenn said," Julie told Luke.

Jenn gave her a dirty look. "And you left just after us because…?"

"I wanted to see if there was a scene after the credits, and there was. I'm guessing there will be a sequel."

"Whatever," Jenn said. "We've got somewhere to be." She dragged Julie away with her.

"Well that was rude," Julie admonished after they'd gotten a few steps away.

"I think he's stalking me," Jenn told her.

"Like you're so stalk-able," Julie replied, jokingly.

"No, for real."

"Oh. Oh shit. What do we do?"

Jenn noticed Julie was including herself in this, and she smiled without realizing it. "Let's go somewhere else," Jenn said. "Somewhere really public."

"There's a new bar downtown that sounds interesting," Julie offered.

"Downtown? Perfect. I'll meet you there." Jenn didn't want either of them to have to come back to the theater to get their car because then Luke would know where they were going to go. Jenn managed to get to the bar and park her car before Julie, so Jenn waited for her outside the bar, trying to look inconspicuous.

"You know, one of these days you're going to get caught with that fake ID," Luke told her.

Jenn looked up from her phone with a jump. "God damnit. What do you want?"

"I'm just here to drink at," Luke looked up at the name of the bar, "Andrew's."

"Bullshit."

"So crude, and after your friend thought so well of me." Luke was really good at pretending to sound hurt.

"What. Do. You. Want?" Jenn spat out.

Luke sighed. "Usually people have questions after their first time seeing magic. I wanted to be around to answer yours."

"I know where to find you," Jenn snapped. "You even made the bouncer give me your card. That's not why you're here. Why are you stalking me?"

Luke sighed. "It's an issue of trust."

"Yeah, I don't trust you at all now," Jenn said. "How did you even track me down?"

"I mean, an issue of trust for me," Luke replied, ignoring her question. "I can't be sure you'll keep my secrets to yourself. I'm keeping an eye on you in case you try to tell someone and ruin this for me."

"Who the hell would I tell?" Jenn snapped. "You're talking about magic! I don't even really believe in it, and I saw it. No one else will believe me if I just tell them. Your secrets are safe, now leave me alone."

"Do you really want me to leave?" Luke smiled seductively.

Jenn pretended not to be affected. "I'm dialing 911 right now. I'm about to call the cops on a creepy older man who's been following me all night," Jenn said, her finger poised over the call button on her phone.

Luke sighed. "Very well. You're no fun." Then he turned around and left.

Jenn sighed and closed her calling app. Even if she had called, Luke would have just left before anyone got to her.

Julie walked up to Jenn. "Hey. I hope you haven't been waiting long."

"No. Let's head in," Jenn said, shaking off her encounter with Luke. This was her scene and it was kind of a game to see how many free drinks she could get.

The bouncer at the door didn't seem to notice their fakes, but he did ask for a cover charge.

"Maybe we can check this out another time," Julie said.

"No, I'll cover you," Jenn said, handing the bouncer the cash.

"Are you sure?" Julie asked.

"Yup," Jenn replied. "Come on." Jenn waited until they were inside before she told Julie that Luke had followed her here as well.

"Seriously?" Julie asked. "Did you call the cops?"

"I threatened to, and then he left," Jenn answered, "but I think he might still be out there."

"Ugh. What a creep. What do you want to do?"

"Let's just stay here for awhile. Maybe he'll give up."

"I hope so," Julie replied, "but if he comes up to you again, call the cops right away." She shivered. "I just need to get the car home so my folks can go to work in the morning."

"No worries. We won't be here that long. Still, if we're going to be here for awhile, we need some drinks. Follow my lead." Jenn strutted up to the bar and Julie followed behind her. Through no coincidence, she ended up next to a man who looked like he had already had a few.

"Hello, ladies," he greeted them, his tongue thick. "Can I get you a drink?"

"Gin and tonic for me," Jenn replied. She pitched her voice higher and opened her eyes a little wider when she was pulling a con like this. She turned to Julie, who struggled to say anything. "She'll have a cosmo," Jenn filled in. They had to keep the momentum going. The bartender nodded and started making their drinks.

"So, what brings you ladies here?" the man asked.

"We've heard Andrew's has the best drinks in town," Jenn replied, giggling.

"That it does," the man replied, saluting Jenn with his drink before taking another sip.

"Here you are," the bartender said, putting their drinks down.

"Thanks," Jenn said with a big grin. She handed Julie her drink and picked up her own.

"So, can I interest either of you ladies in a dance?" the man asked, in what he must have thought was a suave manner.

Jenn giggled. "I couldn't possibly, I might spill my drink. Besides, she gets pretty jealous."

"Jealous?" the man asked.

"Oh yes," Jenn replied. "I'm surprised she's letting me talk to you. Usually my girlfriend wants it to be about us when we go out. She's gotten in so many fights over it." Jenn looked sad. "And she's a black belt so, it never goes well for the poor men."

"No, I-" Julie started to protest.

"I know," Jenn said quickly. "We'll go get a table." She turned back to the man who was now shaking. "Nice to meet you." Then the two of them walked away.

"What was that?" Julie asked.

"What? I just got us free drinks." Jenn sat down a took a sip. "This is pretty good."

"No, I mean, why did I have to be the jealous girlfriend?"

"Oh. It's one of my strategies. I've found guys like the idea of me having a girlfriend, but I have to put the idea of being 'dangerously taken' in there, or else they try to get a threesome. Creeps." Jenn looked up at Julie. "Try your drink."

Julie took a sip.

"You don't drink much, do you?" Jenn asked.

Julie shook her head. "Honestly, I just got the ID so I could see a band. They just had to play in a bar. Anyway, most of the people I see either drink just to get hammered, or don't drink at all."

"Welcome to the happy medium," Jenn said, saluting Julie with her drink.

Julie took a bigger drink of her cosmo. "This is pretty good," she admitted.

"Great," Jenn said. "When we're done with these, I'll get us a few more."

Jenn did manage to get them a few more drinks that night. Most of the time, she maneuvered a man to buy her a drink, but once she tried offering to buy someone else a drink, and then realizing she didn't have any money on her. That one didn't always work, but this time she scored a free drink off of him and left before he realized what had happened.

"Is this how you always get your drinks?" Julie asked. She was on her third drink and was flushed. Jenn figured she probably was as well.

"Most of the time," Jenn replied. "You have to pick out the right person for the con, though. For example, don't go after a couple. If you try the romance angle, one of them might hit on you and cause a big scene. It's better to avoid them. I haven't really tried asking girls, either. It's typical that a guy buys a drink for a girl at a bar, I'm not sure how it works when it's two girls. When you pick a guy, choose one who's a few years older than one you should be dating. So, the kind of guy you like," Jenn teased.

Julie laughed a bit too loudly. "I just think they're hot. I don't want to date them."

"I stand corrected," Jenn replied.

"Although, I do like to date girls a year or two older than me," Julie admitted. She gasped. "Oops."

"I guess that's why you didn't want to pretend to be my jealous girlfriend," Jenn replied.

Julie nodded, still red.

"Duly noted," Jenn said. She shrugged. "Just don't be jealous while you're dating someone and you should be set."

Julie looked at her for a moment, and then laughed, relieved. "Is that your philosophy when you date someone?" she asked.

"I haven't really dated anyone," Jenn answered. "If I'm single, I can do what I like and get these things for free. If I'm dating someone, then I'm limited and I'm sure they'll except things from me."

"I understand," Julie replied, nodding her head sagely. "You're afraid."

"Afraid?" Jenn asked. "This is definitely our last drink," Jenn thought. "Julie's never this blunt."

"Afraid that it won't work. That you'll try to date some guy and he'll end up leaving you. Or a girl. Or whoever. You don't want to fail at it."

"No, people just take too much energy. Besides, you know me. By the first date, I'd be cheating him out of something. By the second, I'd make him think I'm someone else, and I'd break his heart by the third date."

"So you have tried," Julie responded.

Jenn sighed. "Once. I just wanted to see how far it would go. It turns out I was the one who walked away first. He was really clingy."

"Three dates isn't clingy," Julie corrected her. "If you want to hear about clingy, there was this girl I dated in high school-"

"I didn't know you dated any girls in high school," Jenn broke in.

"That's because I was closeted. Now I'm out, mostly. Anyway, she texted me all the time and she wanted to see me every day. When I was at work, she texted me every hour. I swear it was cute at first, but it got to be obnoxious. Who has that much to say?"

"Psycho, clingy lesbians, I guess," Jenn replied.

Julie laughed. "You're funny, but she wasn't too bad. This guy a friend of mine dated was psycho. When they broke up, he trashed her car!"

"Really?"

"Oh yeah. He slashed her tires, broke all the windows, and keyed his name in the paint on the side. But he got the wrong car! She had the same kind of car as her neighbor and he got the neighbor's car instead!"

"Really?" Jenn asked, pondering how she could duplicate this sort of thing. "Sucks to be the neighbor."

"I know!" Julie said. She looked at her phone. "Crap. I've got to go. Good thing I don't work tomorrow."

"I think we'll be all right to leave," Jenn replied. She kept an eye on Julie, but she wasn't wobbly when she stood up or when she walked out. "Maybe it wasn't the booze talking," Jenn mused.

Once they got outside, Julie said, "See you later."

Jenn replied, "See you." They split off to go to their cars. Just before Jenn unlocked her car, she saw Luke across the street. "I'd better take care of this here so he doesn't follow me home," Jenn thought, opening her purse a little bit. She crossed the street and confronted him.

"That was quite a show you put on in there," Luke greeted her. "All for some free drinks. I wonder what you'd do for some real stakes."

"That's the whole point," Jenn replied, annoyed, reaching into her purse. "I get something small and walk away. When the stakes get bigger people get too invested." While she was talking, Jenn whipped her mace out of her purse and sprayed it in Luke's eyes. He tried to grab her hand, but she deftly pulled away and sprayed him again for good measure. "The next time I tell you to leave me alone," Jenn told him, loudly so he could hear her over his yelling, "I expect you to do it."

Then she crossed back to her car, got inside, and drove home.

**

When she woke up the next morning, Jenn realized she would need to get more pepper spray. Her mom had gotten her some when she went to college, but Jenn was sure she never expected it to be used. Jenn decided to stop by a store while she was out breaking and entering in the Velvet Tango Lounge. Jenn smiled at the thought. She'd better get ready quickly so she could get to the bar around lunch time.

Jenn rolled out of bed and pondered her closet. She needed to look cute, but no so cute the construction workers wanted to pursue her. Jenn pulled on a long tank top, and a pair of shorts that had raggedy hems. Her hair was too short to really do anything with it, but Jenn brushed it out until it behaved a bit more. She put in some dangly earrings and looked herself over. It would do. She slid her feet into some strappy wedges, inhaled her breakfast, and was out the door.

It was strange to see campus town so empty during the day. When classes started up again, it would be much harder to drive here, or find a parking spot. Jenn found one close to the Velvet Tango Lounge, but not so close she could see the bar from her car. She didn't want them to know what kind of car she drove in case anyone got suspicious.

Jenn got out of her car and strutted a little down the street. When she saw the construction workers outside of the bar, she gasped a little in surprise and then smiled. "Boy am I glad you're here today!" Jenn said to the first one she saw. "I forgot my wallet behind the bar last night and I need to get it."

"Behind the bar?" the man asked her, looking her up and down.

"I work here," Jenn said, smiling, "and I set down my wallet, and I must not have picked it back up. I'm just going to go in and grab it, if that's all right." Jenn flashed him her most dazzling smile.

"Sure," the man said. "It's all yours until we finish our break."

"Thank you," Jenn said. "I'll be quick." She dashed down the steps to the front door, no easy feat in her wedges, and walked inside confidently. If it was strange to see campus town empty, it was even more strange to see the Velvet Tango Lounge during the day. Where at night it seemed mysterious and suave, it almost seemed overdone in the daylight. Walking quickly, Jenn went to the back wall and found the lock Luke had opened. She wouldn't have much time, but she wanted to at least see what that hallway looked like without him.

Jenn pulled out her bobby pins and stuck them in the lock. As she gently tapped the hook upward, Jenn realized this lock was more complicated than most she had picked. Usually, she was about halfway out of the lock by now. Jenn willed her fingers to work swiftly, but accurately. Finally, Jenn felt the last tumbler click into place and she eagerly turned the lock open. She opened the door.

She was met with a closet full of liquor and cleaning supplies. Jenn stared at it blankly. This was the only door on the wall. There was no way she had picked the wrong place. Why did it open onto a closet instead of a hallway? Jenn heard boots on the stairs outside the door. Quickly, she closed the door and pulled her wallet out of her purse. She smiled and walked to the door just before the worker she'd talked to before came in.

"I found it!" Jenn said. "Thank you so much for letting me in."

"Sure," the man said as she breezed past him.

Jenn walked down the sidewalk back to her car, pretending to be happy, when inside she was fuming. Luke had tricked her again somehow. She definitely had to pay him back for this, but how did he trick her this time? There was no way she had opened the wrong door, but it had led to the wrong place. "Maybe there was a secret switch that moved the closet away," Jenn thought, but she knew she was grasping at straws. There had been nothing odd about it when Luke had opened that door. "Maybe he used magic on it," Jenn thought. Part of her dismissed the thought immediately, but part of her wondered if it was true. Nothing else seemed to make sense, and he did seem to have magic.

Jenn sighed. It was clear that she wasn't getting anywhere trying to go through the bar. She'd have to go back out to the prairie and see what she could find there. Maybe Achi had left another feather helpfully pointing to an entrance to their hideout. "Yeah, and maybe I'll ride a flying pig inside it," Jenn thought, turning on her car.

When she got to the prairie and got out of her car, Jenn immediately went to her trunk to find tennis shoes and a couple of socks. It wouldn't do her any good to cover her feet in blisters by walking too far in her sandals. Miraculously, she found a matching pair of shoes and a pair of socks that were the same color. Jenn pulled them on and got going on the first trail. She looked for any tall rock formations, or even anything at eye level. The first trail turned up nothing.

Sighing, Jenn left the loop, and went onto the second trail, but she was beginning to get tired and hungry. "Maybe I should let Luke keep his damn secrets," Jenn thought, kicking a pebble. It smacked into another, larger rock, and Jenn sat on this rock. She couldn't remember seeing any tall rock formations out here, anyway, but how else would Achi be flying around? Jenn leaned back on the rock she was sitting on, and then it hit her. She'd been going about this all wrong. A cave didn't have to come up above the ground. Achi's entrance might be under the ground. Jenn could have smacked herself.

Hurriedly, Jenn got off the rock and headed back to the first trail. She started at the end and, sure enough, she saw a hole in the tall grass not too far off the trail. Careful not to leave too many bent grass stems behind her, Jenn made her way over there. There was, indeed, a hole in the ground, and it looked like a rock tunnel that came straight up. Jenn slid her fingers around the edge until they caught on something. Jenn snatched her bleeding fingers away but saw one of Achi's feathers was stuck to the rock. "Gotcha," Jenn whispered.

She straightened up, headed back to the path, and began to plan. Since she was going underground, it wouldn't matter what color her helmet was, although she

60

would need a helmet light. It wouldn't really matter whether she climbed it during the day or at night because very little sunlight would get in the cave, but Jenn wanted to climb down at night so no one would get in her way.

Jenn made it back to her car and drove home, trying not to bleed too much on her steering wheel. The cut didn't look that big, but it was bleeding quite a bit. "My mom's going to start worrying about all these bandages on my fingers," Jenn pondered. She realized she should probably put a first-aid kit in her car, or at least a few bandages. She certainly had enough other stuff in there.

When she got home, Jenn ran to their first-aid supply to cover up her cut before she bled on anything. She checked her phone and realized she still had time to get out to the climbing store and get a few practice climbs in before her parents would start to worry. They'd be glad she took up climbing again, either way.

Jenn ate a quick snack and headed out again to withdraw some money from an ATM before she drove out to the climbing store. It was a giant place, part store and part climbing wall, and it was perfect for Jenn's needs today.

Jenn was greeted by a perky redhead behind a desk. "Hello, how may I help you?" she asked.

Jenn decided on a forty-five-minute climbing session. As she was climbing up the wall, with her belayer below, it hit Jenn just how dangerous this could be. She wouldn't have a belayer when she headed into that dark cave at night. She had no real way of knowing what was down there. It could lead to an underground lake. Jenn's foot slipped, and she clung to the wall for one breathless moment before she got her foot back in place again. Then again, if she wanted to have a chance at knowing what Luke was up to, she had to do it. It seemed like he was the only one who could work the door in the bar, but the cave in the prairie was probably a different story.

Jenn reached the top of the wall and began the trip back down. Her trip into the cave would be this easy. She just wasn't sure about coming back out.

Jenn pushed all of these thoughts out of her head as her feet hit the mat. She still had more time on her session, so she chose a different wall, and started climbing up that one.

After she was done, Jenn headed into the store to buy what she was still missing. A helpful employee named Howard came over to check on her.

"I'm doing a traditional night climb," Jenn told him.

"Then you'll probably want a gear sling so you can carry more cams and nuts," Howard said.

"A gear sling?" Jenn asked.

Howard helped her pick one out, and suggested she take a few more cams and nuts as well. Jenn took the longest rope she could, since she wasn't sure how far down the cave went.

It ended up costing a bit more than she'd thought, but Jenn still had plenty of cash to cover everything. "Have a great climb!" her cashier said.

"Thanks," Jenn replied, heading out the door. She still had enough cash and time to stop by her favorite ice cream place. She got a cone of graham cracker ice cream and sat outside to eat it. No one was around, and it was pretty peaceful. It was much nicer than when it was full of people. They all seemed to care about things that Jenn didn't consider important, like who had worn what dress two weeks ago and how good or bad it looked on her. Jenn knew it didn't matter how the dress actually looked, it just mattered what the gossipers thought of the girl. It was much easier to be here by herself. Eventually, Jenn finished her ice cream and left.

Once she got home, Jenn moved all of her climbing gear into the trunk of her car, including a small backpack with some snacks in it. She wouldn't be able to smuggle everything past her parents tonight, and she definitely didn't want them knowing about this. Leah had restrained herself from being too overprotective, but Jenn knew her mother tended to think that way. It was just easier not to tell her.

Jenn told her parents that she was heading out with her friends yet again, and they distractedly waved goodbye to her. Jenn had stayed in some nights this summer and had even spent time with her parents. Those nights, she ended up working on a 3D puzzle with her mom. It was kind of cool, but part of Jenn wanted to knock the puzzle off the table and watch the tiny pieces scatter.

When Jenn got to the park, she pulled on all of her gear except her climbing shoes, which went into her backpack, and her helmet, which she carried under her arm. The park officially closed at dusk, but no one really patrolled it. Jenn started on the trail, and then made her way toward the opening of the cave. It was a little hard to see it at night, but Jenn wasn't willing to use her phone as a light and give herself away. She had put it in her backpack so it wouldn't fall out of her pocket while she climbed. When she got to the cave, Jenn sat down, switched out her shoes, and attached her harness to the rope. Staying low, she found a good anchor point for her rope and tied it off. Then, keeping it nicely in its loops, Jenn tossed her rope down into the hole. She heard it smack into something, but she couldn't be sure if it was just the wall of the cave, or if it was the bottom.

"I'm going to laugh if it's only twenty feet down," Jenn thought as she checked her harness and pulled on her gloves. She adjusted her backpack and put her helmet on. She really didn't know how far down it went. Her rope could be far too short. There was a knot in the end so Jenn wouldn't just slide off, but what if her knot didn't hold? She could die and no one would know where she was.

Jenn shook her head. There was no point in trying to turn back now. She had to find out what else he had down there, and she would be fine anyway. It was just rappelling. Jenn took a deep breath and stood just in front of the edge of the cave with her back to it. Then, she jumped down.

She hit the cave wall again when the top of the hole was just over her head. Jenn clicked her head light on and breathed a small sigh of relief. She could do this. Now that she was in the cave, it didn't seem so bad. Her light bounced crazily as she rappelled down the cave wall, but Jenn managed to find decent footing every time.

"I feel like Alice," Jenn thought, thinking of that character's fall into Wonderland. "Still, I don't think my landing would be as nice as hers if I really did fall."

Jenn had been rappelling forever, and she was starting to worry about what she would do if she ran out of rope. Then, she looked down and saw the floor was right below her. Jenn bounced against the cave wall, and then carefully climbed down. For a moment, she just stood there. Then, Jenn started smiling. She had outsmarted Luke. Pretty quickly, her legs started complaining, so Jenn sat down and took off her backpack. She stretched her legs a bit and ate some of her snacks. Eventually, she switched out her shoes and took off her harness. Jenn decided to leave her backpack there. It wasn't like anyone was around to take it, and it would make walking through the cave easier. Feeling somewhat refreshed, Jenn stood up and started walking.

It was more like a tunnel than a cave. There weren't any branches off of it, just one long corridor. Her headlamp bounced as she walked, making the stalactites and stalagmites jump menacingly. Eventually, Jenn saw some dim light ahead and she clicked off her headlamp. She walked forward slowly, and then crouched to be less visible. There was a long rock wall in front of her, but slightly to the right was a large opening with bright light pouring through.

Jenn army crawled up to the opening and peered through. It took her a moment because she was looking down at it, but Jenn recognized the big room where she had met Achi and Abe. "This must be how Achi gets out," Jenn thought. Jenn looked at the opening in the wall and tried to remember the size of Achi's wingspan. "I guess she would fit through here," Jenn thought dubiously. Shrugging that off, Jenn smiled. She had made it into Luke's cave without him realizing it. She didn't want to get into this room because she would be caught and it was too high to climb down anyway. Jenn slid past the opening, got into a crouch, and continued down the branch of the cave. Not too far ahead of her was another opening in the wall. This one was smaller. Again, Jenn army crawled up and peeked through the hole.

This room was full of stuff that was just tossed around. There was a rusty sword sticking out of the mess, point up, and a mass of gold rings next to a wall. There was a table loaded with what looked like armor. "I wonder if this started out being a useful room," Jenn wondered. "Still, once you've got a few swords lying around, why not throw in a battle axe as well?"

Jenn slid back and shook her head. She had thought Luke would be too fastidious to have a messy room like that. "I bet he knows exactly where everything is in there," Jenn thought, rolling her eyes. There were probably some good things mixed in with the junk but because it was a mess, it was impossible to tell and that would make it harder to steal things. "Or he's just a slob," Jenn thought, shrugging.

She got up into a crouch and continued walking. There was another window in the wall and she wanted to see what this room was. Then Jenn realized she had been hearing a low rumbling noise for a little bit now. She stood up and turned behind her. It was definitely coming from that direction and getting louder. Jenn tightened the strap on her helmet and did a quick inventory of what she had nearby. If she could get into that junk room, she'd have her pick of weapons and junk. Still, Jenn didn't have long until she realized the source of the noise.

A wall of water slammed around the bend and roared toward her. Jenn put her back to the water and ran for it. She needed to find a side passage, somewhere the water wouldn't sweep her up. She needed another of those damn windows to jump through. The fall would hurt less than the water would, but there was nothing. The cave stretched on before her with no turns or windows or anything. Jenn forced her legs to run faster and tried to see where she was putting her feet as her light jumped and skipped all over the place. Then, she felt the water slam into her back and push her forward. Jenn's eyes closed, and she smacked into something. Then everything went dark.

**

Jenn slowly came back to herself, but she hurt all over. It felt like she'd been run over by a truck. She was about to slip back into the nice, comfortable darkness, when someone pressed on her chest. Jenn exhaled sharply and water shot out of her mouth. Jenn rolled over onto her side and coughed out what felt like a gallon of water. She stayed here, retching and shivering for a little bit, grateful for the blanket that was on her. There was a hand rubbing her back as she was coughing. Everywhere that hand touched felt warmer and began to relax, which was nice. Jenn had just about decided to black out again, when a man said, "No you don't. Stay awake." Jenn knew that voice.

Suddenly, Jenn remembered everything. "You tried to kill me!" she accused Luke. She had meant to yell it, but her throat hurt too much and she ended up coughing again. She realized it had been his hand on her back, but he had already removed it, so she decided not to say anything about it. She rolled over to glare at him.

"That was an automatic trap mean to keep anyone from sticking their nose into my business. You're lucky you had a helmet on. It saved your life." Luke sat back on his heels and watched her.

"No thanks to you," Jenn muttered. She pulled the blanket more tightly around her. "Why am I naked? And on the floor?" Her wet hair was plastered against her skull and her face. Briefly, Jenn was glad she kept her hair short so not too much was in her eyes and in her mouth.

"I had to take off your wet clothes so you wouldn't get hypothermia and it would be hard to do CPR if you were on my bed instead." Luke raised an eyebrow at her.

Jenn looked to her left and noticed the wooden bed with jewel green sheets just out of arm's reach. "So, you stripped me before trying to save my life and brought me to your bedroom?" She coughed again and tried to find a way to talk less painfully. "You're messed up." She looked around the room. It was decently sized. The door was to her right. There were two green armchairs facing each other to the left of the door, with a small wooden table in between them. Across from the bed was a wooden wardrobe. Jenn couldn't see past the bed so she didn't know what else was in the room. There was a globe of light up near the ceiling that Jenn didn't pay much attention to. She tried to focus on any of these things to stop herself from freaking out. She didn't want to think about how she had almost just died.

"I had to act pretty quickly since you tried to get yourself killed," Luke said, standing up and moving to one of the chairs. "I took your clothes off by magic while I was giving you CPR."

Jenn glared at him. "And where are my clothes?" If she was angry, then the shaking would go away. Not that she was shaking because she was upset. Jenn told herself she was just cold.

Luke jerked his head toward the corner of his room, near where he was. Jenn's clothes were in a soggy pile.

"Great," Jenn said. "You really are fucked up, you know that?"

"I've been told that," Luke replied evenly.

"So, were you planning on drying my clothes, or do I need to climb out of here in a blanket?" Jenn asked, trying not to shiver too much.

"Let's get you into something warmer first," Luke replied. He stood up and opened a wardrobe. Jenn didn't get a chance to see inside before he closed it and produced a green robe.

"Is everything in here green?" Jenn asked incredulously.

"I don't have to let you wear this," Luke replied.

Jenn snatched it out of his hand. She waited a moment.

"Well, turn around!"

"I've just seen you naked. You realize that, right?"

"That doesn't mean I want it to happen again," Jenn snapped.

Luke sighed and turned around. "This culture really is so uncomfortable with their bodies. What happened to you all?"

"Oh, are you from somewhere else, then?" Jenn blurted, drying herself off with the blanket and then tying the robe tightly around her.

"Yes, but I've been here for some time," Luke answered. "Are you done yet?"

"Yes," Jenn replied, dropping the blanket.

Luke turned around and smiled at her. "You know, I could warm you up more than that robe can."

Jenn took a step back. "No way in Hell." For a moment, she forgot her fear and shock in her outrage.

Luke laughed. "I meant with my magic."

Jenn refused to be baited. She knew what he meant.

Luke shrugged. He walked over to her clothes and picked them up. He put both hands on them and stared at them for a moment.

"Will you stop staring at my panties?" Jenn asked. "It's rude."

"That's not where I was looking," Luke replied, handing her clothes and shoes over to her.

Jenn took them and almost dropped them. They were dry and a little warm. "How did you do that?" she demanded.

"Would you like me to show you?" Luke asked, with a little smile.

Jenn glared at him.

"If you put your clothes on like that, they'll just get wet again and you'll still be cold. You either have to wait here with me until you finish drying off and warm up, or you can let me help you."

"It's warm outside," Jenn pointed out sullenly. She wanted to get home so she could let herself relax and deal with all of this.

"Yes, but it's cold in this cave and you'll be shivering so hard that you'll bite your tongue before you get there," Luke pointed out. "You are the hardest person to help that I've ever met."

Jenn sighed. "Fine." She held out her hand. "Just don't go wandering with your hands."

Luke only smiled and took another step toward her. He held her hand with both of his. Jenn was about to object when she felt the most wonderful warmth fill her hand and start going up her arm. After being so cold, it felt amazing. She could feel her tremors begin to slow and her heart began to slow down to its normal beat. Jenn closed her eyes and leaned into it. She could feel the water drying off of her body and leaving her hair. It was better than a blow dryer. Then, Jenn realized Luke's hand was all the way up at her shoulder, and she jerked away, the sleeve of the robe falling back down over her arm.

"I told you not to do that," Jenn snapped. It was hard being snapped back to reality like that, but she throttled her emotions down.

Luke gave her a look and started to say something. Then, she could see him change his mind and say instead, "You only said not to wander. Not what that meant."

Jenn shook her head but didn't have the energy to fight him this time. "Well, now that I'm dry and my clothes are dry, I'm ready to leave. Turn around so I can change."

"Again?" Luke asked. He looked at Jenn's face for a moment. "Very well," he replied. "You really are touchy about that."

"I'm not in the habit of being naked around men I've maced," Jenn growled, pulling her panties and shorts on under the robe so she showed as little skin as possible. Then she turned around to get into her bra and shirt. She sat on his bed to pull on her socks and set the robe on the bed next to her. "I'm done," Jenn announced. She began tying her shoes.

"Can I ask what you were doing sneaking into my house at night?" Luke asked, turning around slowly.

"Of course you can ask," Jenn said, switching shoes. She finished tying the other one in silence.

Luke sighed. "If you wanted another tour, all you had to do was ask."

"Let's just make this clear: I don't trust you. I don't like you. I know you're up to something and I know it's not good." Jenn stood up.

Luke smiled at her. "My dear, I'm sure many would say the same about you."

Jenn was already dealing with a tumult of emotions, so his insult barely made a dent. "How do I get back the way I came in?" she asked instead.

"You mean through the hole in the ground in the prairie?" Luke smiled at her. "It wasn't hard to figure out. What I want to know is how someone who denies that she has magic was able to get through all of the wardings placed there."

"Maybe your wardings just ran out of power," Jenn replied. She looked over at the wall and noticed a hole near the top. "Is that where you brought me in?" she asked, pointing.

"Yes," Luke said. "You had washed quite a ways down the passageway before I got to you."

"How come the water didn't come in here?"

"I told it not to," Luke replied.

Jenn looked at him for a moment, then sighed. "Do you use magic to solve all of your problems?"

"Only when I'm not using it to create problems for others," Luke answered. "Now, would you like me to get you back to the prairie, or do you want to walk through the bar with no ID?"

"Wait. The prairie is on the other side of town from the bar. How does this cave connect to both of them?"

"It doesn't," Luke replied. "I'm sure you found that out when you tried to break in through the bar the other day."

"How does that door lead two places?" Jenn demanded. She should have expected that he knew what she had been up to.

"A door can lead many places if you know how to open it," Luke replied cryptically. He held out his hand. "So, would you like me to take you back to the prairie?"

As much as Jenn didn't want him to touch her right now, she didn't want to go through the bar and have to figure out how to get to her car. "Fine," she said holding out her hand.

Luke smiled and slid his hand onto hers. Then he pulled her close and they rose above the ground. Even though she hated that he was the one touching her, part of Jenn was glad to have someone holding her close after she almost died. Again, Jenn pushed her emotions away. She still wasn't safe to deal with all of that. They moved slowly through the window into the upper hallway and the light followed them.

"What is that?" Jenn asked, tensing.

"It's a will o' the wisp," Luke replied. "They usually live in marshes, but I convinced a few to live here and light up the caves for us."

"Convinced, huh?" Jenn asked. Then they were whizzing down the hallway and Jenn didn't want to talk any more. She loved the feeling of flying, even if Luke were there with her. They turned sharply down the corridor and Jenn found herself at the bottom of the shaft she'd rappelled down.

Luke set them gently on the floor and Jenn stepped away from him opened up her backpack. Everything was still there and dry. "The water didn't come up here either?" Jenn asked.

"It would be too loud here and might draw attention," Luke replied.

"Oh, of course," Jenn said. "Well, thank you for bringing me here, I guess."

"Are you planning on climbing back out?"

"Yes," Jenn replied, pulling on her harness. She realized it was dumb, but what else was she supposed to do?

"It really would be much safer if I brought you out."

Jenn considered for a moment. She would be climbing unfamiliar territory in the dark with no light and no helmet. She was exhausted and bruised and her muscles were tired and shaky. It wouldn't be a good idea. Even though she wanted to fight him on this, she just didn't have the energy. Jenn sighed and stepped out of her harness.

"That is, unless you'd like a personal tour of my home?" Luke asked.

"The point was to see it without you there," Jenn replied. "It wouldn't really make sense to see it with you." Besides, she had a pretty good idea he would end that tour would in his bed.

"You really don't like me, do you?" Luke asked.

"You undermined me the first time we met and yelled at me for something I don't have. Then you stalked me, tried to kill me-"

"It was automatic. I didn't turn that on."

"-stripped me down without my permission-"

"Saving your life," Luke interjected.

"-taunted me, interrupted me, and now you're asking if I like you?"

"I did also save your life and open your eyes to the world of magic," Luke pointed out.

"Which I don't have," Jenn asserted.

"You seem to get along with it well enough."

"Whatever. The point is that, no, I don't like you. You're a con man and I don't appreciate it when you try to con me."

"I should have recognized someone else in the trade," Luke replied with a smile and a small bow.

Jenn bit off a curse and pulled on her backpack. "Just get me out of this place," she growled.

"Of course," Luke said, offering his hand.

Rolling her eyes, Julie grabbed his hand and let him wrap his other arm around her waist. They shot up the shaft and soon their feet were gently landing on the ground. Jenn stepped away from Luke and he let her go. He waved his fingers and Jenn's rope shot out of the shaft, untied from her anchor point, and coiled itself neatly at her feet.

"I would ask that you don't use this way to visit me again," Luke requested. "There are other traps and it's a mercy you didn't set any of them off."

Jenn didn't reply. She just bent down and picked up her rope.

"Jenn, all of the traps in there are meant to kill intruders. Please tell me you won't come back in that way unless I'm with you."

"Why are you traps set to kill people?" Jenn demanded. "Why would you do that?"

"I have made some powerful enemies and, while my precautions might not kill them, they will certainly slow them down."

Jenn looked at him. "More magic users?" she asked.

"In a way," Luke replied evasively.

Jenn shook her head. "Fine. I won't come back this way to break into your house. Why do you care if I die so much anyway?"

"Because, whether you believe it or not, there is a strong power in you and I'd like to see you master it."

Jenn raised an eyebrow at him. "Are you trying to compliment me with that somehow?"

"I'm merely stating the truth."

"Whatever," Jenn snapped. "I'm going home." She turned around and started walking back toward her car.

"Very well. Good night."

Jenn flipped him off over her shoulder and didn't bother to turn around and see his reaction. She made it back to her car and focused on driving back home. It was late, so there was no one else on the road. She slipped into the house without seeing her parents and focused on getting into her room and closing the door. Then she sat on her bed and grabbed a pillow.

Now that she wasn't in immediate danger any more, or dealing with Luke, Jenn let herself go into shock. Her whole body shook and she began to cry, pushing her face into the pillow to muffle the sounds. She sat like that for awhile, shoulders heaving and holding the pillow so tightly it hurt her arms. Finally, after what seemed like hours, Jenn felt herself begin to relax and to breathe more slowly. She wanted a hot bath to relax in, but Jenn didn't want to be in any more water right now. She settled for sliding under the covers in her bed and leaning against her headboard.

Jenn grabbed her phone to do something mindless, anything, so she could think about something else before she went to sleep. Briefly, Jenn wondered what Julie would say if she heard about Jenn's night. "She'd probably ask me how I ended up naked in some man's bedroom," Jenn thought. She started laughing at the absurdity of it and did her best to muffle her laughter, but she couldn't stop. She laughed until she cried again and Jenn pulled the tissue box closer until she was done. Then, Jenn grabbed her tablet, plugged in her headphones, and put on one of her favorite shows. She watched it until she finally fell asleep.

**

Jenn woke up with a start and immediately regretted it. If she thought she was sore yesterday, today was even worse. Jenn groaned and slowly sat up. She was still in yesterday's clothes. Jenn levered herself out of bed and noticed there was an earring on her pillow. The other one wasn't in her ear, or in her hair. It was probably lost in Luke's cave somewhere. Jenn shook her head and looked in the mirror. She looked terrible. Her makeup was smeared across her face and her hair looked like a bird's nest. Jenn cleaned off her makeup first and noticed a small bruise beginning on her jaw. "Great," she thought. She'd have to think up an excuse for that.

Then Jenn sat down and began slowly combing her hair. She couldn't remember it ever being this tangled before. Eventually, she was done and Jenn carefully combed through her hair one more time to make sure she had gotten all the tangles out. Then she stood up and stretched, wincing. This was going to be a long day.

Inevitably, her mind went back to the previous night. She started to wonder about Luke's junk room. She wondered if the pile of rings was actually gold rings. "Can't be," Jenn thought. "If he had that much money, why would he live in a cave?" She had to be missing something here. "And why does he have a battle axe?" Jenn wondered. Luke didn't look like the sort who would choose to solve his problems with violence. Unless he wasn't able to talk his way out of it. Briefly, Jenn wondered how good Luke was at fighting. He didn't look strong enough to use that axe well, but he had surprised her before.

Annoyed that she was still thinking about him, Jenn stood up and went to get herself some breakfast. As she ate, she looked at her phone and realized she had missed a call. It was from Julie. Curious, Jenn listened to the voicemail.

"Hey, Jenn. This is Julie. I need to talk to you about something. My shift ends at 3:20. Can you meet me for some coffee? Text me back. I can't talk on my phone except on a break. Bye."

"Interesting," Jenn thought. She wondered what Julie wanted to talk to her about. Her treacherous mind wondered if it was something about Luke. "I'll meet you at Royal Latte at 3:30," Jenn texted Julie. They had met there for coffee before and Jenn knew it was right next to Julie's diner. Jenn finished her breakfast and put her dishes in the dishwasher. She had some time before she needed to get ready, so she decided to do a little yoga. Her mom had dragged her to a few classes so Jenn remembered some of the basic poses. She just wanted her muscles to hurt less. Strangely, her left arm wasn't sore at all. That had been the arm Luke had touched when he dried her with magic. Jenn snapped this thought off before it could go farther and instead she leaned further into the pose.

"I wonder how my voice sounds," Jenn said. Her throat felt a little scratchy, but nowhere near what it had felt the night before. That was a relief at least. Jenn dressed carefully and put on her makeup to hide the bruise on her chin. At least it looked small and not too bad. It would be hard to explain a purple blotch on her face. Eventually, it was time to go, so Jenn grabbed her purse and headed out.

Jenn had a tradition at Royal Latte of giving bogus names to the cashier for her drink. Today, she used Indefatigable. The barista gave her a strange look but didn't ask. Jenn wondered if she was getting a rep with them. As Jenn waited for her drink, she looked around for Julie's long, black hair, but didn't see it. "I guess she's not here yet," Jenn thought. Julie was probably working past the end of her shift.

"Indi-fat-igbull," a barista said uncertainly.

"That's me," Jenn said, walking up to get her drink. She grabbed a small table in the back and sat down to wait for Julie. She didn't have to wait too long. Julie walked in, saw Jenn, and headed straight over. "Hey," Jenn greeted her.

"You shouldn't mess with the baristas," Julie said. "They almost spit in your drink."

"What?" Jenn asked, looking at her drink. "How do you know?"

"I can read minds," Julie told her.

Jenn laughed. "That's a good one. I haven't used that trick in years."

"I'm serious," Julie replied, stone-faced. "At first, I thought it was kind of a hangover or something, but it's still happening today." She paused for a moment. "Yes, I know you like to think about pink rhinos or something stupid when you ask someone to read your mind. Don't bother to ask me."

"This is going to be a one-sided conversation if you respond to what I'm thinking before I can speak," Jenn said. This was crazy. She hadn't thought Julie would be one for pranks, but maybe there was something to what she was saying.

"Of course there's something to it," Julie replied. She sighed and looked at the couple sitting near them. "He's about to break up with her."

"Really?" Jenn asked, looking at them.

Julie nodded. "It's stupid because she'll definitely move across the country for him, but he can't bring himself to ask because he thinks she'll say no. So, he's planning on breaking up with her instead."

"Wow. You should be a couple's counselor," Jenn replied. "I guess she really can read minds," Jenn thought. She had seen magic in action once, after all. Who was to say it couldn't happen again? Still, this was pretty strange.

"You've seen magic before?" Julie asked, her attention fully on Jenn. "When?"

Jenn sighed. "It was from that asshole stalker, Luke." She thought about the first time she'd gone into his cave and tried not to think about the previous night at all.

"Wow. That's crazy," Julie replied. A look came across her face. "What aren't you thinking about here?"

"If I wanted you to know, I'd think about it," Jenn said, still trying to block it out, but having trouble doing that while she was talking.

"Oh my God," Julie said. "Are you okay?"

"I'm fine," Jenn said, realizing she wasn't going to be able to stop her friend. "I'm just a little sore."

"Well, I knew that part. You've been thinking about being sore this whole time, but I didn't know you almost died! And Luke saved you."

"And was an ass," Jenn added.

Julie nodded. "He seems to do both to you. I wonder why that is."

"I'm sure he's desperately in love with me, but too crazy to be able to show it in a normal way," Jenn answered sarcastically.

Julie looked thoughtful.

"That wasn't meant to be realistic," Jenn snapped. "Of course he's not in love with me. The man is old enough to be my father and he doesn't like me."

"He doesn't like that you're poking around in his stuff," Julie said. "That's very different." She took a deep breath. "Sorry, but I've got to say something." She got up and went to the table with the couple. "Hi," she said. "Don't break up with her. Tell her about your job and ask her to move in with you. You're totally ready for that."

Jenn got up to save Julie from herself. "Sorry," Jenn said. "She's a couple's counselor and she can't stand to see people give up." Jenn dragged Julie away. Jenn was a little annoyed to leave her drink behind, but maybe it was for the best.

"Sorry," Julie said.

"It's fine," Jenn replied, knowing Julie was thinking about the drink too. They stood outside the café to talk. "Is it better out here?" Jenn asked.

Julie nodded. "It's easier when people are further away. So, I know you hate Luke, but do you think he could help me? I'm pretty desperate."

"I'm not sure," Jenn replied, thinking, "but I bet Abe could. He's a teacher of all sorts of things."

Julie gasped, probably at Jenn's mental picture. "He's a merman! Abgal, sorry. What's an abgal?"

Jenn shrugged. "Abe, I guess."

"How circular of you," Julie replied dryly. "So, can we go today?"

"Sure, but we'll have to wait until tonight," Jenn told her. "We'll go in through a bar."

"Through a door that only leads to a cave when Luke opens it. Jenn, what have you gotten mixed up in?"

"I'm trying not to be," Jenn snapped, "but you had to drag me back into it."

Julie's face fell for a moment and then she looked a little happy. "You really don't want to see him again, but you'll take me anyway?"

"Well," Jenn replied. She couldn't think of anything to say to that, but she couldn't leave Julie like this.

"Thank you," Julie told her sincerely.

"You're welcome," Jenn replied. "So, uh, I'll pick you up around 8? I think the bar is open by then."

"Sounds good," Julie said. "I think I'll go for a run until then or something. Somewhere I can get away from all of the voices."

Jenn nodded slowly. "My life has definitely gotten weird this summer," she said.

"Mine too," Julie replied. "See you tonight."

Jenn nodded. She walked away and got in her car. She looked over and saw Julie walking to the diner's parking lot. Just to mess with Julie, Jenn thought, "Wow. She's got a great butt."

Julie stopped and Jenn could imagine her face getting red. Julie turned around, with a blush like Jenn expected, and shook her head at Jenn. Then Julie turned away and continued walking to her car. Laughing, Jenn turned on her car and headed home. If she used it right, it was a lot easier to mess with Julie now that she was a mind-reader.

Jenn spent the next few hours pretending that she wasn't going back to see Luke that night. She really didn't want to see him again, and damn the part of her that remembered how his hands had made her feel warm and relaxed. Of course, soon after she remembered this, Jenn remembered how she had been fighting not to go into shock when she was with him. She couldn't trust him when she was feeling vulnerable. She had to remember that.

Even Leah commented on how grumpy Jenn was during dinner. "Is everything okay?" Leah asked.

Jenn bit off her first answer. "It's all right," she said. "I'm kind of in a fight with someone and I'm going to see him tonight."

"Why?" Mark asked.

Jenn shrugged. "He's helping another friend with something and I have to be there. It's just dumb drama."

"Well, honey, if you're not comfortable, then you don't have to go," Leah told her, sounding worried.

"No, it's fine," Jenn said. "I just don't want to talk to him is all."

"If he gives you any trouble, you know what to do, right?" Leah asked.

"Yes, Mom." Jenn had listened to her mother's advice about self-defense with mixed emotions. Leah had demonstrated a few moves for her as well. Jenn didn't think she would need them, but she had paid attention to humor her mother.

"So why are you going?" Mark asked.

"I just need to be there," Jenn said. "It's kind of complicated and I don't want to get into all of it, but it'll be fine. All right?"

"All right," Leah said, when Mark opened his mouth to ask another question. Mark closed his mouth and ate another forkful instead. "Do you know when you're coming home tonight?"

Jenn knew the question within that question. She wanted to know when they should start worrying about her if she wasn't home. "Not really," she said truthfully. "I'll text you if anything comes up, okay?"

"All right," Leah replied, not really convinced, but willing to let it drop. Jenn was glad that she had finally trained her mother to drop things.

Jenn helped put away the leftovers and went in her room to stew for a bit. She wished there was anyone else she could take Julie to, but anyone else would think Julie was hearing voices and try to medicate her. Somehow, Jenn would bet this was all Luke's fault, but she couldn't say how. Jenn pulled out the knife made from Achi's feather and looked at the blade for a moment. "I suppose I believe in magic," she thought. She sheathed the blade and put it in her purse. Then she waved goodbye to her parents and headed out to get Julie.

When Jenn pulled up at Julie's house, Julie was already halfway to the car. She got in and put on her seatbelt. "I could hear you coming," Julie said, "and yes, it is getting worse."

"Should I turn up the radio?" Jenn asked.

"No," Julie said. "That would make it worse."

"Oh," Jenn replied. "I'll get us there as fast as I can."

"Thank you," Julie replied.

"You've got to stop saying that to me," Jenn said, looking at the road.

"Why? Because no one else does?" Julie waited for a moment. "Why would you think no one else would trust you with something like this? There's got to be someone else who trusts you."

"How about you stay out of my mind?" Jenn asked, her hands gripping the wheel.

"Sorry," Julie said. She looked out the window and didn't say a word the rest of the trip.

Jenn was pretty sure that Julie was still reading her mind but just wasn't saying anything about it. Of course, thinking that meant Julie knew, but Jenn decided not to say anything about it anyway. This was getting to be more annoying than Jenn had hoped for.

Soon enough, they parked and headed down to the bar.

"Yes, I've got my fake," Julie said quietly to Jenn.

Jenn sighed and nodded. They came up to the bouncer. He nodded Jenn through without checking her. He stopped Julie and looked at her ID for a moment. Then he nodded and let her go through.

Jenn guided them to a table near the bar because it was brightly lit.

"Why didn't he check you?" Julie asked after they sat down.

"I think he remembers everyone who's ever come in here," Jenn replied. "He only checked my ID the first time I came here."

"Weird," Julie said. She looked a little pained. "Keep talking. Give me something else to focus on."

Jenn cast around for ideas. "Do you have your classes picked out for next semester?"

"Of course," Julie replied. "I'm starting to take more social work classes, which is good, but I've got a few gen eds I couldn't test out of. You?"

"General management. I've got an English class as one of my gen eds, too."

Julie laughed. "I feel bad for that professor. You argued with our English teacher about everything."

"But I always found something to back it up in the text, so he had to give me points for it," Jenn replied with a smirk.

"You did that on purpose," Julie said.

"Only every time." Jenn shrugged. "Some people just can't take a good argument."

"And some of us can," Luke said.

Jenn felt herself tensing immediately as he put a hand on her shoulder. She stopped herself from tearing his hand away and instead she gently removed it.

"Luke, this is my friend, Julie."

"Hello," Julie said.

"Pleased to meet you again," Luke said, taking her hand and kissing the back of it.

Jenn almost felt better that he tried to charm the pants off of every girl. Almost. "She needs your help. Can we talk in your cave?"

"Any friend of yours is a friend of mine," Luke said expansively.

"Right," Jenn replied sarcastically, getting up.

They walked over to the door and Jenn watched Luke open it to see if there was a trick to it. It looked like he just unlocked the lock and opened the door. The three of them walked into a cave and Luke shut the door behind them.

"So," he said, "what seems to be the trouble?"

"I'm a mind-reader," Julie blurted. She looked at him strangely for a moment. "But I can't read your mind."

"No, you wouldn't be able to," Luke said.

"How did you do that?" Julie asked.

"Practice. I can help you not to read everyone else's mind. I'm assuming that's why you're here?" He turned to Jenn.

"I couldn't think of anyone else who could help," Jenn muttered.

"My dear, I'm here to help anyone learn their magic better."

Jenn wished that Luke didn't say "my dear" quite so warmly when he spoke to her.

"Thank you," Julie said, drawing Luke's attention back to her. "I was worried I was going to go crazy."

"Many people do when this happens to them," Luke said, walking down the hall. Jenn and Julie fell into step next to him. Jenn wasn't sure how Luke ended up in the middle, but she didn't like it.

"Oh," Julie replied quietly.

"Don't worry," Luke said. "There's not too many people around here, so it should be easier for you to think."

Julie smiled. "You're right." Then she looked confused. "But the bar is right down this hallway. I don't feel anything from over there."

"You wouldn't," Luke replied.

"Oh," Julie said.

Jenn was pretty sure Julie had just read her mind about how they were now under the prairie, but Julie didn't say and that was probably for the best.

Luke stopped and opened the door to the big cavern where Achi lived.

"Wow," Julie said. "It's just like you remembered it, Jenn."

"You couldn't keep her out of your mind?" Luke asked Jenn, raising one eyebrow.

Jenn immediately felt inferior. "No. It's not like I've ever needed to before."

"I suppose not," Luke said, but Jenn still felt like she had fallen short of his expectation for her. And she was mad that part of her cared.

Luke introduced Julie to Achi and Abe. Abe declared that Luke would be better able to help Julie learn her powers and that he needed to go. "We're having a big event tonight," he said mysteriously.

"Then we won't keep you," Luke said.

Abe slid under the water and was gone.

Jenn looked at the water to make sure he wasn't there. Luke grabbed her right arm to turn her around and his grip was just enough to hurt Jenn's sore muscle. Jenn flinched and Luke immediately let go. "If you're not feeling well, I can help you feel better," he offered with a smile.

"I'm fine," Jenn snapped. "Just sore from your death trap."

"I did apologize for that," Luke replied.

"You really didn't," Jenn told him. She glanced at Julie. "Whatever. We're here to help her."

"Of course," Luke replied. "I was thinking the two of you should help each other."

"Okay," Julie said.

"It must be really bad for her to be this desperate," Jenn thought. Then she remembered Julie was reading her thoughts. Julie gave Jenn a strained smile.

"Julie, I'd like you to start by focusing on reading only Jenn's mind."

"Why me?" Jenn asked.

"Because you're here anyway, so you may as well be useful," Luke replied. He turned back to Julie. "After you get the hang of reading just her mind, you can try to read no one's mind."

"Why don't I just start there?" Julie asked.

"It's easier to take it down to one mind first," Luke replied. "So, focus on only reading Jenn's mind."

Julie looked at Jenn and the focus she brought to bear was almost frightening. Jenn looked her in the eye for awhile until that got uncomfortable. Then she looked away, but that was almost worse. Of course, Julie knew all about Jenn's discomfort and that only made Jenn more annoyed. Still, this was helping Julie.

After awhile, Luke said, "I think you've got the hang of that. Very good. Now, try to read no one's mind. It's a little like meditating."

"Okay." Julie sounded unsure. She closed her eyes.

Jenn looked at her. It was strange to feel so much concentration, but not get the piercing stare that went with it.

"I heard that," Julie said.

"Aren't you supposed to not be reading my mind?" Jenn asked.

Julie sighed. Jenn decided to think about Julie in detail just to annoy her. Julie's eyes had a particular shape to them that Jenn hadn't seen anywhere else, even in Julie's siblings. When they were open, Julie's eyes were filled with a happiness and life Jenn usually only saw in children. Julie seemed to glow through her skin and she had a knack for making your problems seem much more manageable, while offering the right amount of sympathy with her facial expressions. Jenn wasn't sure how she did that. Julie's hair was long, black, and a little coarse. Occasionally, Julie would braid it back, but she usually just put it in a ponytail when it was getting in her way. At the moment, it was loose and spilled over her shoulders onto her chest. Julie's boobs were pretty small, as they went, but Jenn supposed they were proportional to Julie's body.

Jenn looked at her friend's face for any kind of reaction, but she didn't see one. "She must be doing well not to react to that," Jenn thought. Still, Jenn wasn't done with her assessment. Julie was a little under average height and as skinny as she had been in high school when she'd been on the soccer team. Jenn wondered if Julie was still as strong as she had been then. Doing stadium runs will give you great legs, which probably also gave Julie a great butt. Jenn looked down Julie's legs to her feet in sandals and noticed what looked like a simple drawing of a flower on Julie's left foot. Jenn wondered if it was a tattoo and if so, what Julie's parents had said about it.

Julie's eyes opened. "I did it!" she exclaimed. Then her face fell. "Oh, the thoughts are coming back in again."

"That takes a little practice for it to be automatic," Luke replied. "Still, you're doing very well for your first lesson."

"You're not doing much," Jenn accused.

"Everyone has their own way of doing these things," Luke explained. "If I tried to tell Julie in detail what to do, it probably wouldn't be the way most comfortable for her and it would take her much longer."

"I guess," Jenn replied, not terribly convinced.

"Now, the next step is to try to read someone's mind who is actively resisting," Luke continued. He turned to Julie. "Would you like to rest before we try this?"

Julie smiled a little uncertainly. "I think I would," she said.

"Probably a good idea," Luke replied. He gestured to the set of outdoor furniture near the lake. They all sat down in white metal chairs around a white metal table that had a hole in the middle for an umbrella.

"Is all of your furniture this nice?" Jenn asked, rubbing off a little of the rust.

"Of course not. Don't you remember the furniture in my bedroom?" Jenn wanted to punch that smirk off of Luke's face, but he started speaking again before she could say anything. "Sometimes the guests here don't know how to interact with human furniture," Luke explained. "I found it's best to put in something sturdy." He smiled at Jenn. "Can I get either of you something to drink?"

"What have you got?" Julie inquired.

Luke smiled and got up. "Mostly wine," he said, looking at the cavern wall in front of him. There were many small holes and Jenn could just see the tops of wine bottles sticking out of most of them.

"You use the rock as a refrigerator?" Jenn asked.

"Of course," Luke replied. "It's far easier than trying to get electricity in here."

Jenn had to admit he had a point. "Probably best to get a Moscato," Jenn said. "Julie likes sweet drinks."

Julie nodded and glanced at Jenn while Luke was turned around. Jenn shrugged. She had no problem drinking while they were in here as long as she didn't drink too much.

"Although you don't like sweet drinks," Luke pointed out to Jenn, coming back to the table with a bottle and three glasses.

Jenn shrugged. "It'll do."

Luke poured them all a bit too much and set the wine bottle down. "To good beginnings," he said, holding his cup up.

"What beginning?" Jenn asked, not clinking her glass just yet.

"The beginning of Julie learning to use her power," Luke replied with a smile.

"Sure," Jenn replied. It was just a toast, after all. She clinked her glass with the other two and waited for Luke to drink first.

After his first drink, Luke put his glass down and smiled. "Jenn, I promised that no harm would come to you while you were in here. Do you not trust that promise?"

"Just making sure," Jenn replied. She took a sip of her wine. It was an excellent Moscato. Damn him.

"I know what will make you feel better," Luke said. He turned to Julie and looked into her eyes. "I promise that no harm will come to you while you are here," he told her.

Julie blinked rapidly. "Thank you," she managed.

Luke smiled and turned his attention back to both of them. It was almost like Julie had been in a spotlight before and Jenn wondered if he had done that to her the first time he promised her safety.

"So, ladies," he said. "While we're taking a break, tell me about yourselves."

"Oh, I'd rather hear about you," Jenn said with a very fake smile.

"Very well," Luke replied. "I came here many years ago to find a better life. I certainly found it. I've got a good life for myself and I'm able to live off of the interest of the money I've invested, which gives me plenty of time to help others with their magic. I've seen what happens when I'm too late and the results can be devastating. The magic user will sometimes go mad and destroy everyone close to them." Luke shook his head sadly.

Jenn looked over at Julie. Julie's hand was gripping the arm of her chair so hard her knuckles were white and her lips were pressed into a thin line. Jenn gently put her hand on top of Julie's and Jenn could feel Julie's hand relaxing under her. Jenn took her hand back after a moment.

"Thanks for that," Jenn told Luke sarcastically.

"You asked to hear about me," Luke replied, "and that is my life's work."

"Great," Jenn replied, rolling her eyes. "I didn't hear the part where you are a con man."

"Oh, my dear," Luke answered. "Everyone uses everyone else, it's just about how good you are at doing it."

"That's not right." Julie argued, still tense.

"Oh?" Luke asked.

"I'm studying to be a social worker. You don't go into a broken home and try to help because you want something from the people there."

"Of course you do," Luke answered, looking confused. "It helps your reputation to be able to save a situation that looks dire. If you can keep the child in their home, it gives you less paperwork, while easing your conscious about how they now have a safe place to live, and helping others is something that you do to feel better about yourself."

Julie opened her mouth and shut it again. "How can you have so little faith in people?"

"I'm sorry," Luke replied, sounding genuine. "It's been awhile since I've talked with someone who has as much faith in them as you do."

"You don't think I have faith in people?" Jenn challenged.

Luke smiled. "You clearly don't trust me," he pointed out.

"You've given me every reason not to," Jenn shot back.

"But I think you have some faith in people still," Luke continued, "for now, anyway."

"What do you mean by that?" Jenn asked.

"I'm sure Luke was just trying to annoy you," Julie said smoothly. "Right, Luke?"

"Oh, Julie. Half the fun of talking to Jenn is annoying her." Luke shot a smile at Jenn that made her stomach flip. Jenn glared back. "I can tell that you're an only child," Luke told her.

"The miracle baby," Jenn agreed sarcastically.

"Miracle?" Luke asked.

"Never mind," Jenn said, drinking some more wine. "So, how does it work to block someone from reading your mind?"

"That depends on the person doing the blocking," Luke replied, letting Jenn's abrupt topic change go by without comment.

"You never give a straight answer, do you?" Jenn asked.

"No," Luke replied with a grin.

Jenn realized Julie had rested her hand on top of Jenn's. Jenn realized that now she had the arm of her chair in a death grip. Slowly, Jenn relaxed her hand.

"I'm ready to try it if you are," Julie said to Jenn.

"Sure," Jenn said. "I guess I just go with whatever?"

"Whatever seems the best way to you," Luke agreed.

"Great," Jenn replied, settling herself in her chair. "Okay, go ahead." She imagined her mind in a big safe. The door swung shut and the lock twirled. There was no getting in.

"A safe?" Julie asked almost immediately. "You know that wasn't the right way to go."

"Fine," Jenn replied, closing her eyes. She imagined a padlock on her mind, clicking shut. The key was far away.

"A padlock?" Julie asked. "Now you're just thinking about where you would hide a key for it. Huh. Some interesting places."

"One more time," Jenn demanded.

"All right," Julie agreed.

Jenn imagined her mind erased. There was nothing to find so it was impossible to read her mind.

"Wow," Julie said after a moment. "You did it. I can't even tell that you're here!"

"Really?" Jenn asked, opening her eyes.

"Oh, there you are," Julie said, opening her eyes as well.

Jenn frowned and looked toward Luke. His chair was empty. It made Jenn uncomfortable to realize he had gotten up and she hadn't noticed. A quick glance around told her that he wasn't in the cave. "Don't say anything," Jenn thought at Julie. "Let's go see where he went."

Julie looked around and raised an eyebrow at Jenn.

"Come on!" Jenn thought at her, standing up.

Rolling her eyes, Julie stood up as well and they walked to the door. Quietly, they walked into the hallway. Jenn left the door just a little bit open behind them so they could get back inside quickly. Jenn had seen the room to the left of the big cave and there wasn't a door anywhere close on the right side, so she went to the door across the hall. She put her ear up to it for a moment and didn't hear anything. Jenn eased the door open, being as quiet as possible. It looked kind of like their high school chemistry lab.

Jenn and Julie looked at each other. "Why does he have a lab?" Jenn wondered. Julie shrugged. Jenn pulled the door shut carefully and moved down the hall to the room across from the junk room. She put her ear to the door and heard a man talking. "Come listen," Jenn thought at Julie.

Julie frowned at Jenn, but then put her ear to the door as well.

"...find them," the man said. He sounded angry.

"I have been looking," Luke replied defensively.

Jenn immediately wanted to know who this other man was.

"You have not been looking hard enough. Do not let me find out that you were the one who hid them," the man threatened.

"I'd be careful threatening me," Luke retorted.

"Why?" the other man asked. "You've already put yourself back in a cave. All I have to do is keep you here and bring the serpent, but we would need to bring back your wife to tend to you. Where is she?"

"She's out exploring the worlds," Luke replied, "something I could be doing if I wasn't stuck here."

"Once you find Huginn and Muninn, then you will be able to join her," the man stated, "but you will need to find them quickly. We are growing impatient."

"Remember that the last time you chained me in a cave, I brought about Ragnarök and I can do it again," Luke promised, pronouncing the strange word easily.

"You waste my time," the man said. "When I come back, you had better have them."

"Of course, brother," Luke replied sarcastically. "Anything for you."

"We've got to go," Jenn thought at Julie. They both quickly but quietly moved away from the door and back into the big cave. "Let's look at Achi," Jenn thought at Julie. "The table's too far."

Jenn very carefully pet Achi's head. After Jenn's fingers had left, Achi shook herself and preened her chest. Small, metal feathers fell to the floor.

"Her beak must be strong," Julie said.

"Luke never told me what they do when she molts," Jenn said.

"We use a rolling magnet and a lot of patience," Luke said from behind them.

"Where did you go?" Jenn asked.

"My family is in town and I had to take care of something," Luke said.

"Your family?" Julie asked. "Do they live here?"

"No, they mostly stay in the old country," Luke said, with a slight smile.

"It must be hard being so far away," Julie commiserated.

"That's actually part of the reason I came here," Luke said with a tight smile. "I'm the black sheep of the family, if you can even call it a family." He looked at Jenn. "So, how did you and Julie do?"

"Jenn managed to hide her mind," Julie answered with a smile.

"Ah, good," Luke said. "Only someone with magic can do that, you know," he said to Jenn.

Jenn sighed. "I have yet to see this "magic" I have do anything for me."

"Ah, so whatever brought you back to me to talk about magic was a bad thing. I had wondered about that. Do you need my help setting it right?" He put a little emphasis on the last few words.

Jenn stiffened. Her mind went back to a dinner conversation with her parents a few days ago. Apparently, Perdita had broken her arm when climbing somewhere she shouldn't have been. The doctors were having a lot of trouble setting it right because she kept compulsively climbing with it. Luke had used the exact phrase Leah had when talking about it. "How does that bastard know?" Jenn thought. Next to her, Julie flinched.

"That bad, huh?" Luke asked, looking at Julie.

"What?" Julie asked, a little flustered.

"Whatever Jenn was just thinking about. Jenn, I didn't realize what a good poker face you have. Unfortunately for you, Julie's poker face is terrible."

"It's nothing." Julie was a terrible liar and Jenn realized that Julie was still reading her mind when Julie's face flushed.

"If I want your help with anything, I will ask you for it," Jenn told Luke very clearly.

"Feel free to. I want to help you, Jenn." He sounded so sincere.

Jenn felt shivers go up her back when he said her name, but she hid it the best she could.

Luke looked between Julie and Jenn for a moment. "I think that might be all for tonight, ladies. Unless you'd like to help me finish the bottle of wine we opened?"

"We'd better go," Jenn replied flatly.

"Very well," Luke said with a smile. "Let me walk you to the door." He placed a hand on the small of Jenn's back to steer her to the door of the cave, but Jenn dislodged his had with the back of her arm. "My apologies," Luke said.

"I don't understand why you're always trying to touch me," Jenn complained. Ahead of them, Julie opened the door to the cave and stepped into the hallway.

Luke smiled at her. "Perhaps I can't help myself."

"What a terrifying answer," Jenn snapped, walking through the door ahead of him. "I would hope a man of your age would have a little self-control."

"If you don't want me to touch you anymore, I will try to stop," Luke told her, pulling the cave door shut behind him. "It is a habit, but I will do my best to break it for you."

"Good," Jenn snapped walking down the hallway.

"Do you think you'll be able to get through tomorrow?" Luke inquired of Julie.

"I think so," Julie said, with a shaky smile. "Today was terrible, but I had no idea how to stop it, or if I was crazy." She gulped and Jenn immediately slowed her stride so she wasn't quite so far ahead of Julie. "But now that I have a strategy, I think tomorrow will be better."

"Good," Luke said. "You've got to go one day at a time with something like this. If you want something to help you sleep, may I recommend these?" He pulled a bottle out of his pocket.

"No," Jenn stated before Julie could answer.

Luke laughed. "You truly don't trust me. Julie, if you want some melatonin, you can buy it most places. It's the best one I've found for those just coming into their power if they have trouble sleeping."

"Thank you," Julie said, not making a move toward Luke.

They came to the end of the hallway. "Good night, ladies," Luke said, smiling at both of them. "I would recommend you come back tomorrow night so Julie can work on her training some more."

"Can't we train without you?" Jenn asked.

Luke laughed. "I suppose you could, but my cave is far from other people, which should make it easier, and if something goes wrong, I can step in and stop it."

"Goes wrong?" Julie asked. "Like what?"

"I don't want to give you ideas about what could happen, but you will be perfectly safe trying to only read your own mind tomorrow, Julie."

Julie sighed a little and nodded.

"Fine," Jenn said. "We'll be back tomorrow night."

"Thank you," Luke replied. "Good night, ladies."

"Good night," Julie replied.

Jenn said nothing. Luke opened the door and Julie walked through first.

"Jenn?" Luke asked, grabbing her arm.

Jenn stopped and looked at him. He was awfully close.

"I wish you would reconsider my offer. I could be a great one-on-one teacher for you."

Jenn savagely ignored the tingling in her stomach and shook Luke's hand off of her arm. "Good night," she told him flatly and walked away.

Jenn was fuming as she and Julie left the bar and walked to Jenn's car.

"So," Julie said once they were inside the car, "do you love Luke or hate him?"

"What?" Jenn yelled.

"Do you love him or hate him? You're all prickly when you're talking to him, but when he touches you or says your name, you start getting flustered."

"Probably why the bastard keeps touching me," Jenn muttered. She looked at Julie. "Why would I love him? He stalked me. I maced him so he would stop."

"You wouldn't be the first person to love an abuser," Julie pointed out.

"Do not put me with your charity cases," Jenn snapped. She looked away before she could see how hurt Julie was. "OK, I will admit to you that he does something to me when he's around, but I don't trust him, or like seeing him. He's probably using magic on me." Something occurred to Jenn and she tried to phrase it gently. "Was he trying to seduce you, do you think?"

Julie laughed a little. "I was wondering when you were going to ask. I'm not sure. There were subtle things and a few hints dropped. I thought I was off of men, but I might reconsider for him."

"Even knowing how terrible he is?" Jenn asked, flabbergasted.

Julie laughed. "Oh, no. I think he flirts with everyone, but you especially. He might be using some magic with it, I couldn't really tell you, but I can tell you're important to him and I wanted to know if it went both ways."

"I'm what?" Jenn asked, confused. "Why do you think I'm important to him? All I do is yell at him and he just hits on me to make me more mad."

"There's small things," Julie said. "I, um, you know I can't help but read your mind, right?"

Jenn sighed. "Yes."

"Well, you were thinking about the night you drowned and he pulled you out. When you were coughing up water and he was rubbing your back, you know he was using magic to help warm and relax you, right?"

Jenn considered, knowing Julie could see if she was lying. "I suppose he was."

"But he didn't say anything about it and he moved his hand away when you moved. I think there's something there, but you could also be right that he's a con man. Just because you're important to him, doesn't mean he won't use you."

"You're quite the romantic," Jenn said.

Julie shrugged. "I've only started studying social work, but you see all kinds at the diner and I've heard more than my share of tough life stories."

Jenn took a deep breath and tried to calm herself down. She started the car.

"Oh, and Jenn?" Julie put her hand lightly on Jenn's shoulder.

"Yes?" Jenn asked, looking at her.

"Now I understand just how much he messes with you, so thank you so much for taking me to Luke anyway. I really needed the help and just knowing I'm not crazy makes me feel so much better." Julie squeezed Jenn's shoulder and dropped her hand. "I'll try not to read your mind on the way home," Julie promised.

Jenn smiled. "I appreciate that," she said.

They drove in silence for awhile. "What was up with huggin' and muggin'?" Julie asked.

"Huginn and Muninn," Jenn corrected idly. "I'm not sure, but Luke certainly has a history with that guy. What do you think ragnarock is?"

"I have no idea," Julie said. "I kind of wish I could read Luke's mind, but even if I could get past his shields, he would definitely know."

"And that would probably cause more problems than it would solve," Jenn mused, turning onto Julie's street. "I'll do some research tonight."

"Great," Julie replied. "We actually have some melatonin for Katrina. She had some trouble sleeping awhile ago."

Jenn remembered that Katrina was Julie's younger sister. She was about Perdita's age. Jenn tensed, remembering how Perdita couldn't stop climbing on things now. She couldn't help but feel responsible, even though the idea that Jenn had done something was stupid. Jenn stopped in front of Julie's house. "Well," she said.

"Jenn? I know I said I'd try not to read your mind, but… What happened with Perdita?"

Jenn sighed. "I…Can we talk about this later?"

"Sure," Julie replied immediately. "Of course we can. I'll see you tomorrow night?"

"I'll be here," Jenn replied with a smile. She held up a finger. "And don't thank me again. I'm getting sick of hearing it."

Julie laughed. "Then I'll just say I appreciate it. See you tomorrow night."

"Bye," Jenn replied. She waited until Julie got into her house and then drove away. It was going to be a lot harder to be so private with Julie listening in on everything. The reasons Jenn had trained herself to have such a good poker face were so she wouldn't give away a prank and so people didn't butt into her business. She was going to have to practice blocking Julie's mind reading once she got home.

Of course, once she got home, Leah wanted to know how it had gone. "Was that jerk able to help your friend?"

Jenn smiled. It was kind of funny to hear her mom call Luke a jerk in such an off-handed way. "He was," Jenn said.

"Oh good. Did you need to smack him so he would help?"

Jenn laughed. "No. It was fine." Now that she was home, Jenn could almost pretend Luke didn't exist. It was weird having a double life. "Is that your latest puzzle?"

"Oh yes," Leah replied, smiling. "It's going to be a duck when I'm done."

Jenn looked at it. There was certainly a lot of yellow on the table, but she couldn't see how it would become a duck.

"Do you want to help me with it?" Leah asked.

Jenn knew her mom would ask her more about this jerk if she did. Jenn felt better now, but she didn't want to get into why Luke was such a jerk with her mom. "I wonder if she thinks I like him too," Jenn pondered. "Sorry, but there's something I need to look up."

"Doing research over the summer?" Leah asked, mock surprised.

"I know," Jenn replied sadly. "What is this world coming to?"

Leah laughed. "Well, if you want to help later, I'll be here."

"All right, Mom," Jenn replied. As Jenn walked to her room, she saw her dad was staring at his laptop and typing intently. It looked like he had another long night of work ahead of him. Sometimes Jenn wondered about whether he lived to work or worked to live.

Once she got in her room and shut the door, Jenn dropped onto her bed and pulled open her laptop. She tried searching for Huggin and Muninn. She found out it was actually Huginn and Muninn and they were two characters from Norse mythology. "What the hell?" Jenn asked. The man she'd heard speaking to Luke had to have been speaking in code about something else, but just in case it was important, Jenn read the article about Huginn and Muninn anyway. They were ravens who told Odin what was happening in Midgard, which was Earth. Huginn meant "thought" and Muninn meant "memory".

"Maybe it's some kind of spying device," Jenn pondered. There was no way the man in that room was looking for a couple of ravens. Whatever he needed was incredibly important to him and that man was powerful enough to worry Luke. Jenn sighed. "If only I had seen that guy. He definitely knows more about Luke." Jenn glanced at her clock. She tried searching for Huginn and Muninn to see if she could find anything else, but the only results were about Norse mythology.

Then Jenn tried to search for ragnorock. She got a bunch of music at first, but after she changed the spelling to Ragnaröck, she found something else. "More Norse mythology?" Jenn wondered. This was about the end of the world. The gods and the giants fought and everyone died, except two humans who hid in the world tree and repopulated the world. "Gross," Jenn thought. "I don't want to think about how their kids had more kids."

Jenn looked away from her laptop. It was weird how focused Luke and his visitor were on Norse mythology. It had to all be code for something. "I can't believe that Luke would actually be able to end the world," Jenn thought, "and he said he had caused it, so they can't have really meant the end of the world. It must have been the end of something else." Something else jumped out in Jenn's memory. "Luke said he had been chained in a cave." Jenn puzzled for a moment. "That can't be right. No one chains people up in caves. We have prisons now. Besides, if this guy did chain Luke up in a cave, you can be sure Luke wouldn't be helping him. He'd be conning him."

It was a lot to think about, especially after dealing with Luke and using energy to keep Julie out of her mind.

Giving up for the night, Jenn called up one of her shows on her laptop and watched that until she fell asleep.

**

When Jenn woke up the next morning, she had a headache. "Probably from the magic I used last night," she thought. Then she finished waking up. "I don't have magic," Jenn muttered to herself, getting out of bed. This was going to be a long day and remembering that she was going to see Luke that night just made it longer. Jenn decided to read more about Norse mythology to pass the time until then.

She learned that Odin had one eye because he sacrificed the other one so he could learn to read runes. They were the gods of the Vikings and they were definitely centered around war, but the stories didn't really tell her much. Thor was strong and dumb. The dwarves were good at making magical things. Freya was the goddess of love and kind of a slut. The gods and giants hated each other, but still managed to make Loki.

Loki was half giant and half god and far more interesting than the rest of the gods. He played tricks on them whenever he was bored, so the other gods didn't really like him. One night, Loki cut off Thor's wife's hair. Just because he felt like it. Loki ended up going to the dwarves to get replacement hair for the woman because, apparently, she couldn't just wait for it to grow out. While he was there, Loki convinced the dwarves that the gods wanted to have a contest to see which group of the dwarves could make the coolest stuff. If one group won, they would get to cut off Loki's head, so of course Loki tried to sabotage them. They still won, but before they could cut off Loki's head, he pointed out that they couldn't harm his neck. Annoyed, the dwarves sewed his mouth shut and left. "Ouch," Jenn thought. Still, because of Loki, the gods got a lot of cool stuff like a golden ring that dropped more golden rings, a golden boar, and Thor's hammer. Loki had gotten himself into a huge problem, but he had talked his way out and ended up a bit better off than before. "He's better at that than I am," Jenn thought.

She checked the clock and remembered that she had to water the plants before her mom got home from work. Sighing, Jenn got up to find the hose.

**

That night, Jenn started to tell Julie what she found out, but Julie got excited and read Jenn's mind to see all of it. "You really like this Loki character," Julie remarked.

Jenn laughed. "I should take notes on how to trick people. He goes for high stakes."

"Yes, he does," Julie replied. "Please don't do that."

Jenn laughed. "Hey, I'm a college student in the middle of a corn field. What chance do I have to mess something up that badly?"

"The corn fields are, like, twenty minutes away," Julie corrected her. Then she laughed. "I guess you're right. So, you think Hugin and Munnin are code names for something?"

"Well, they can't be Odin's ravens," Jenn replied. "I can believe in magic, I guess, but Norse gods is taking it a bit too far. Don't you think?"

"I don't know," Julie replied. "The ravens might exist even if the gods don't."

Jenn shrugged. "So, how was work today?"

"Better," Julie said. "Although, I did write down a girl's order and walk away before she could say it."

"Oops," Jenn said.

"Yeah," Julie replied. "She was very confused when her food came out."

"I'll bet." Jenn realized something. "You could work in a fair as a mind-reader."

"You mean a freak show? No thank you. I'll stick with the diner."

"If you must," Jenn replied, mock sighing. She pulled into a parking space near the Velvet Tango Lounge and sat for a moment.

"Are you all right?" Julie asked.

"I guess so," Jenn said. "He just gets under my skin, you know. And don't you dare say we don't need to come back. He might have been lying about you causing devastation, but he might not have been. We are not taking that chance."

"Okay," Julie replied. "I thought I was the mind-reader, not you."

"I'm very good at predicting what people will do," Jenn said.

"Really?" Julie asked. "I'm sure you are."

Jenn shrugged. "How else could I trick people? Anyway, we'd better get in there before I drive away."

Julie laughed and they both got out of the car. This time, the bouncer didn't check either of their IDs and Luke was waiting for them at the bar.

"Ladies," he said, nodding to them.

"Hello," Julie replied.

Jenn said nothing.

Luke smiled at her. "Shall we?" he asked. He got up and they went through the door into the cave. This lesson was very similar to the first, except that both Jenn and Julie were much better. As the lessons continued and they got better, they visited Luke less often, which was good for Jenn's blood pressure. It got to the point where Julie could manage not to read anyone's mind unless she got too flustered. Similarly, Jenn could keep Julie out of her mind unless she was too flustered. Although, with Luke around, it didn't take much to make Jenn flustered. Once they mastered the basics, Luke began having Julie categorize the minds around her and sort out who was who. Jenn tried to sneak away while they were having these lessons, but Luke was vigilant and didn't let her get far by herself.

"There's a lot of people who seem...normal," Julie said after one lesson, "and there's some who seem like me, with just a bit of something else."

"Probably magic," Luke supplied.

Julie nodded. "But I see what you mean about Jenn. She's full of magic one minute and then almost normal the next."

"Glad to hear I'm almost normal," Jenn replied.

Julie gave her a look. "You know what I mean." She turned back to Luke. "I've felt a few minds like yours as well…"

"Best to tread lightly there," Luke advised. "Not everyone is as nice as I am."

Jenn guffawed and Luke gave her a heart-stopping smile. Jenn rolled her eyes and looked away, trying to stop her stomach from doing flips again.

Once their college classes started again, Jenn and Julie went to the Velvet Tango Lounge less often. Jenn managed to go with Julie a few times a week, but sometimes Charles, Emma, and Helen decided they wanted to go out and Jenn always went with them. Julie called their lessons with Luke their double life and said they both needed some time off from it anyway.

One night when they managed to have a lesson, Jenn and Julie were doing very well. Jenn was able to ignore Luke almost completely and was much better at hiding her mind than usual. Julie was trying to read her mind with little success. Jenn could feel the effort in the air and knew that one of them would have to give sooner or later, but this time it would be Julie. Apparently, Julie did not agree because Jenn could feel the pressure on her mind increase. She fought back, trying to blank her mind and slide out of Julie's grasp. She had almost slipped away when something snapped in her mind and Jenn saw a white light everywhere. She heard someone screaming and then the bright whiteness changed to darkness, but she was not unconscious.

Jenn felt herself begin to fall, but someone caught her. It was a man and he was mumbling foreign sounding words quickly and desperately, gently stroking the hair off of her face. Jenn felt her awareness coming back. It felt nice to have someone stroking her hair like that, and Jenn smiled. She opened her eyes and saw Luke's face over hers. His eyes were huge and his face had gone white.

"What happened?" Jenn asked, struggling to sit up. Her throat was sore and Jenn realized she had been the one screaming. In a flash, Luke's face was completely different. Now he looked like nothing special had happened.

"Julie discovered how to attack someone with her magic," Luke replied, helping Jenn sit up.

"Oh my God," Julie said, crouching next to Jenn. "I'm so sorry. Are you okay?"

"I'm fine," Jenn said, looking at Julie, although she was still reeling. She turned to look at Luke. "I guess having you around is a good thing sometimes." Jenn was very well aware that something terrible would have happened to her if he hadn't stepped in. Still, she shrugged him off and sat there by herself for a moment. It began to hit her what could have happened to her. Jenn started shaking, but she was damned if she was going to cry in front of Luke.

"Let me get you a blanket," Luke said quickly.

Jenn watched him leave and realized she was already starting to cry. "Damn it," she said.

Julie held her hand and looked into Jenn's face. "Did it hurt?" Julie asked carefully.

Jenn shook her head but wasn't able to smile like she wanted to.

Julie nodded slowly. "Do you remember when you convinced the low brass that you were an undercover cop?"

Jenn barked out a laugh around her shivers. She knew what Julie was doing, but she went along with it. "And that they had to give me all of their weed?"

"Did they?" Julie asked.

"Of course, they did," Jenn replied, smiling. "You're not looking at an amateur here." She wiped the tears off of her cheeks and took a few deep breaths, slowing her heart down. "Tommy was the worst, though. He kept bringing me pot for, like, a week afterwards."

"What?" Julie asked laughing.

"Oh yeah," Jenn said. "He had so much that he didn't want to carry it all at once, so he'd bring me a bag here and there." Jenn laughed.

"And I'm sure you did something responsible with all of that weed," Julie mock lectured.

Jenn laughed and sat up a bit straighter. "Of course, I turned it in to the administration. Well, most of it."

"Didn't you just put it in the principal's desk?" Julie asked.

"Hey, I didn't call the cops on him or anything. I just left a note saying that he should restock the vending machines once in awhile."

Julie laughed and shook her head. "You are a trouble-maker," she said.

Jenn beamed at her. "That's why I'm so popular," she said sarcastically.

Julie shrugged. "I like you well enough."

"As do I," Luke said, walking back over with the green blanket from his bed. He draped it around Jenn.

"You've got to stop putting this blanket on me when something traumatic happens to me here," Jenn told him. "I'm going to start associating this blanket with trauma."

Luke looked at her for a moment, assessing, and then laughed. "Well, we can't have that, can we?" he asked. "I'd like you to be comfortable in my sheets."

Jenn felt herself blushing. "You really need to get laid," she told him.

"I agree," he said, looking at Jenn and smiling. Jenn wasn't sure how to react. Her stomach seemed to have dropped and she felt tingly, but in a different way.

"So," Julie said loudly. They both looked at her. "What did you mean attack?"

"Ah," Luke said. He sat down on the ground next to Jenn, facing Julie. "Sometimes, that's part of a mind-reader's gift, is mental attack and defense. I wasn't sure if you would have it or not."

"Is that a good thing?" Julie asked.

"It means you're strong," Luke told her. "There might be other applications of your power lurking in your mind."

"You make it sound so comforting," Jenn cut in.

"Lurking just means we need to draw her powers out," Luke clarified.

"I think I'd like to focus on the ones I know about for now," Julie chimed in. "If we go pulling all of my power out, I don't think it could handle it."

"Wise decision," Luke agreed. "For now, when we work on controlling your mental attack, you can use me as your target."

"Because your mind is so much stronger than mine?" Jenn asked.

"More or less," Luke replied, shrugging.

Jenn just sighed and shook her head. She was pretty sure this was true and she wasn't up to arguing with him about it. After awhile, Jenn stopped shaking and she set the blanket aside. Then she and Julie left.

"Take care," Luke said to Jenn at the end of the hallway. "If you start to feel strange, call me."

"Strange?" Jenn asked.

"You'll know what I mean. If something doesn't seem right, call me and I'll come help you."

"Yeah, like I want you coming to my dorm."

"Promise me," Luke said, earnest.

"OK. God," Jenn replied. "I'll call you if I start to feel weird."

Luke smiled. "Thank you. You still have my card, right?"

"Tattooed over my heart," Jenn shot back. "Good bye."

Jenn and Julie walked to Jenn's car in silence. They got in and put on their seatbelts.

"I'm sorry," Julie said.

Jenn looked at her. "You didn't know that could happen. Hell, I think even Luke was surprised." Jenn tried to forget how worried he'd looked when she first opened her eyes.

Of course, Julie was reading Jenn's mind and she gasped when Jenn tried to forget about this. "He really looked that worried?" Julie asked.

"Yes," Jenn replied grumpily. Since Julie was in her mind anyway, Jenn replayed the whole bit with Luke desperately mumbling and gently brushing her hair away from her face.

"That's so sweet," Julie said. "What is with him?"

"I have no idea, but I think it would take several therapists to get to the bottom of it," Jenn said, starting her car.

"Do you still think he's just trying to use you?" Julie asked.

"Yep," Jenn replied, pulling onto the street. She knew that Julie knew that moment with Luke would stay with her for awhile, but that didn't mean Jenn had to like it. They didn't talk the rest of the way to Julie's house.

"See you later," Julie said, getting out of the car.

"Bye," Jenn replied with a smile. She waited until Julie made it into her house and then she drove away, deep in thought.

Their lessons continued after that, but only rarely did Julie practice attacking Luke's mind. Jenn wondered if he was worried, or if he was just trying to keep Jenn from wandering off. Still, he seemed to be more focused on Julie finding others with "the gift" as he called it than anything else.

Some nights she spent learning about magic, but Jenn still went out with her friends on other nights. One particular night, they were walking down the main street, Jenn was cursing herself for not breaking in her heels earlier. "Hey, we've never been there," Helen said, pointing at the Velvet Tango Lounge.

"I dunno," Jenn said. "I hear their drinks are lousy, and I don't think it's a dancing bar."

"Great," Helen said, "My feet hurt."

"Mine too," Emma said.

"I can't believe I wore these shoes," Charles joked.

Jenn remembered that he was wearing sandals. She raised an eyebrow at him.

"I can't help it if there's a double standard about men wearing heels," Charles said with a grin.

"There's other bars," Jenn began, but Helen was already starting down the stairs. With a sigh, Jenn put herself at the back of the group so none of them would notice that the bouncer didn't check her ID, and she managed to put them at a table in a dimly lit part of the room. Hopefully, Luke wasn't here tonight.

A waiter came over and handed them all menus. After he walked away, Helen joked, "Is this a menu or a book?"

"I think it's cool," Emma said. "I've never seen drinks like these."

"As long as they have scotch," Charles said, setting his menu down.

The waiter came back soon enough. Charles was confused when he was offered a few different kinds of scotch. Jenn was pretty sure he picked one at random. Helen asked for a Bloody Mary, sticking with what she knew. Emma got a blackberry fizz, and Jenn ordered the Ninth Ward to see what that drink was like.

They had a bit of time before the waiter brought their drinks back and Jenn was starting to relax. It was silly to think Luke would be here every night. They started talking about their summers and Helen talked about her vacation in France.

"So, there I was swimming in the waves off the coast of France," Helen began. "One of them pulled me under and I came up coughing a bit. Then this gorgeous French guy picked me up and carried me back to the beach. When I say he was strong, I mean he was ripped!"

"But you weren't in danger," Jenn interjected.

"I know that, but he was hot, so who cares?" Helen asked.

"What's his name?" Emma asked.

"Raphael," Helen said.

Jenn only heard girls say a name like that shortly before they gushed about how great he was. Funny, but those relationships usually didn't last long.

"We had a wonderful time," Helen said. Jenn knew what that meant.

"You know, that's a common way for men to pick up rich girls," Jenn said.

"What?" Helen asked.

"Oh yeah. I'm sure you wore a designer swimsuit and he could tell."

"You know I did, but I didn't buy anything for him. It was just a fling and we both knew it." Helen shrugged. "I know you're trying to mess with me, but I don't care. He was hot, it was fun, and I'll probably never see him again."

"Too bad. He sounds so dreamy," Charles said.

Helen laughed. "I don't think you're his type."

Charles made a lot of jokes about being gay. Jenn hadn't figured out yet if Charles was joking, or if he was serious and he just didn't want to say so. Maybe that was why the love triangle she tried to set up between the three of them fell through. Well, that and none of them believed her bullshit.

The waiter came back with their drinks and they were all quiet for a moment to enjoy them.

"This is fantastic," Helen said.

"Mmhm," Emma said, setting her blackberry fizz back down.

"They mixed it just right," Charles said.

"Charles, that's just scotch and ice," Helen pointed out.

"I know," Charles said, "but they did it was such artistry."

"We'll have to come back here," Emma said.

Damn it. If they came back here again, it was only a matter of time until they ran into Luke and Jenn did not want to mix those parts of her life. She felt a tap on her shoulder. "Speak of the devil," Jenn thought.

"I hope I'm not intruding," Luke said, "but it's good to see you relaxing with your friends, Jenn."

At least he hadn't called her "my dear". "Thanks," Jenn replied coldly.

"Do you know Jenn?" Helen asked, always on the hunt.

"Oh yes," Luke said. "We met this summer."

"I'm Helen," Helen said, "and this is Emma and Charles."

"Pleased to meet you," Luke said, smiling at all of them. Jenn felt validated when both Emma and Helen turned red after that smile. Charles just smiled back, so it was hard to tell what he thought.

"Don't you have something to do?" Jenn asked Luke pointedly.

"Oh, you know me," he replied. His smile for her was just a little different than his smile for her friends.

"Grudgingly," Jenn said. "Good bye."

"So lovely to meet all of you," Luke said. "Please enjoy the drinks, I'll get the bill for all of you."

"You really don't have to do that," Jenn stated.

"I insist," Luke replied. "Have a good evening." He sailed away before Jenn could say anything else.

"I hate that guy," she mumbled.

"Why?" Helen asked. "He's a catch! Nothing wrong with an older man, especially if he has money."

Jenn rolled her eyes and sighed. She didn't want to begin to list all of the problems she had with Luke. "He's an asshole and he's just pretending to be nice so all of you like him."

"I like any man who buys me a drink," Charles said.

"That's all it takes, huh?" Jenn asked.

Charles shrugged. "Depends on the man, I guess."

"He did seem nice," Emma said.

"Whatever," Jenn replied.

"Jenn, you seem awfully uncomfortable here. Have you two ever…?" Helen trailed off to let Jenn fill in the blank for herself.

"No," Jenn snapped. "I don't waste my time on men like him."

"It seems like you don't waste your time on anyone," Helen replied. "You really should sometime."

"Do we have to talk about this right now?" Jenn asked.

"I'm just trying to help you out," Helen said. "He's probably great in bed."

Jenn closed her eyes and counted to ten. She'd heard that was supposed to help.

"So," Emma said quickly, "Helen, have you found anyone interesting in your classes so far?"

"God bless the peacekeepers," Jenn thought as Helen began prattling on about the latest group of guys she was considering sleeping with. At least she was easy to sidetrack. After they left the bar, Jenn drifted to the back of the group and Charles drifted back to her.

"Hey, are you okay?" he asked.

"I'm fine." Jenn realized this would be more believable if she hadn't snapped at Charles.

"Has Luke ever…has he done something to you? You don't have to tell me what it was, but… It seems like he hurt you."

Jenn was taken aback. She had never thought Charles would be trying to ask her if she'd been sexually assaulted. "No," she said. "No, nothing like that. I mean, he followed me once, but I maced him in the eyes so…"

"Damn," Charles replied. "Are you worried about him? Can I help?"

For a moment, Jenn tried to imagine Charles giving Luke a serious talking to. There were many ways that could go, but most of them ended with Charles' dignity in tatters. "No, it's fine. He's just an asshole and he likes to upset me."

"Sounds like it's not fine."

"I know," Jenn replied. "I know. Believe me, Julie tells me the same thing."

"Julie? She's the one who's majoring in social work, right?"

Jenn nodded.

"Then she probably knows more about this than I do. I know you can take care of yourself, but if you need something, or if you think he'll only listen to a guy, you let me know, okay?"

"Sure," Jenn said, remembering the times she or the other two had pretended that Charles was their boyfriend when they'd been out. There was once both

Helen and Emma had been pretending that Charles was their boyfriend to keep two guys away. Jenn had laughed and then stepped in to pretend to be Helen's girlfriend and punched the guy bothering her in the face. They'd had to leave the bar after that, but it was worth it.

Jenn and Charles caught back up to Emma and Helen. "I think I'm going back to my dorm," Jenn said.

"It's still early," Helen protested.

"I know, but I'm pretty tired. I'll see you guys later, okay?" Jenn asked.

"See ya," Helen replied.

"Good night," Emma said.

"Do you want me to walk you back?" Charles asked.

Jenn shook her head and smiled. "No. I'm fine. It's not far. Bye." Jenn took the walk back to her dorm to clear her head. If she was going to keep seeing Luke, and it seemed like she was, then she had to get over her reaction to him. She knew part of the reason he kept heckling her was because she responded so strongly, but that didn't make it easier to stop. Still, she could trick him by suddenly becoming disinterested. Maybe that was the way to look at this. If she stopped responding, he would probably stop being so over the top and that could solve the problem. Probably. Sighing, Jenn unlocked her dorm room and started getting ready for bed.

**

The next morning, Jenn saw Hank on the quad. "Hey," she greeted him. "I never see you here."

"My class got cancelled today so I thought I'd head out here to study," Hank explained, smiling.

"Nice," Jenn said.

"Oh, did you hear about Perdita?" Hank asked.

"I heard that her arm wouldn't heal right," Jenn said cautiously.

"Now it will. Just the other day when Mom and Dad took her to the doctor again, there was a man there who said he could help her compulsion."

"Really?" Jenn asked. Most people who said things like that were liars, and she knew Starla and Daryl didn't have money to spare on fakers.

"It actually worked after just one session!" Hank cheered. "She's back to herself, maybe a little braver, but she's not climbing on everything anymore."

"That's great!" Jenn said with a smile. The guilt she had been carrying began to ease. Even if she had caused this, it was fixed now.

"Oh yes, Dr. Luke is a miracle worker."

"What was his name?" Jenn asked, her spine turning to ice.

"Dr. Luke. He said he likes people to call him by his first name."

"Oh. Was he blonde, about so tall?" Jenn asked.

"Yes. Do you know him?"

"I think I might," Jenn replied cautiously.

"Then please thank him again for us. He didn't even charge for it. Mom and Dad tried to pay him, but he wouldn't take their money."

"Really?" Jenn asked, her anger rising.

"Really, really," Hank said with a smile.

"That's great," Jenn said, lying through her teeth. "I'll see you around."

"Bye," Hank said. He was humming as he walked away.

Jenn knew there was no way she could get into Luke's cave until that evening, so she spent the rest of the day trying to avoid people and snapping at anyone who talked to her. Jenn and Julie weren't planning on another training session tonight, but Jenn stomped down to the Velvet Tango Lounge that night anyway. She had barely walked in the door when Luke came over and guided her back to his cave. Jenn didn't want to make a scene in a bar where everyone would likely take his side, so she waited until the door was closed behind them in the cave hallway.

"Now then, my dear, what seems to be the trouble?" Luke asked calmly.

"He's going to play it cool, is he?" Jenn wondered. "Stay the hell away from my family," Jenn spat.

"Excuse me?" Luke asked.

"Stay away from them. I don't know how you found Perdita, but you will never talk to her or anyone else in my family ever again."

"But what if your parents want to meet me?" Luke asked with a grin.

Jenn slapped him across the face. Luke staggered backward. It felt good, so Jenn did it again. She raised her hand a third time, but Luke grabbed both of her arms and shoved her back against the cave wall. Jenn hadn't realized how strong he was before. She held onto her anger so she wouldn't be terrified.

"I asked if you wanted my help and you refused, but you weren't doing anything to help her," Luke explained, speaking very distinctly. "It was holding you back and making you never want to try magic again. I had to do something."

"You didn't have to do a damn thing. You went behind my back and did something to my cousin. You should have left it alone."

"I was helping you and it was not easy. It took me a lot of effort to undo that wish."

"I don't care how hard it was. You weren't helping," Jenn snapped. "You were changing things in my life without asking. Do you know how violating that is?"

"You want to talk to me about violation?" Luke asked, leaning in closer. His anger was bubbling over, too. His hair went from light blond to dark black and his skin began to glow. His face began to look horribly scarred. "About someone hurting your family? Be my guest because, my dear, I can top anything you can say to me."

Jenn glared at him, trying to ignore his change in appearance. "I don't know what happened to you and I don't care. Don't you dare pull that shit again. You've hurt my family and you're hurting me. I've had enough of you."

Luke looked briefly confused and stepped back a pace. He slowly let go of Jenn's arms. As he did, his glow faded until he looked the same as he always had. Jenn put her arms down and started massaging the life back into them. She really hoped he hadn't bruised her and that he couldn't see her shaking.

"I was trying to help you," Luke told her firmly.

"Next time, talk to me first. Except," Jenn considered, "I never want to see your face again."

"Please," Luke said, putting his hand quickly on the wall in front of Jenn. She flinched and he hastily moved his hand. "I don't do well with violence," he said quietly. "My dear, you are the last person I want to hurt."

"Probably because you want me for something," Jenn grumbled, stepping around him.

"Now why would you think that?" Luke asked.

"Because you keep deflecting when I bring it up," Jenn said. She straightened her back and looked him in the eye. "Goodbye, Luke. Julie and I will not be coming back."

"Jenn," Luke said, "you can't deny that you have power and you're going to need help harnessing it."

"Not from you," Jenn interjected.

Luke looked at her for a moment and deflated a little. "If you ever change your mind, please come find me," Luke said.

Jenn looked down at her red forearms. "I'm good, thanks." She stepped past Luke to open the door, and she left.

**

Jenn made it back to her dorm room to a note from her roommate. She was staying at her boyfriend's place tonight again, although it was hard for Jenn to read the note through the tears in her eyes. "Thank God," Jenn said, falling onto her bed. She started shaking and distantly thought that this was the third time she'd gone into shock since this summer. Jenn grabbed her pillow so no one would hear her crying. Her phone started buzzing and, by habit, Jenn checked to see who was calling. It was Julie. Taking a deep breath, Jenn answered. "Hello?"

"Hey, Jenn. I know we're not scheduled to meet with Luke tonight, but I was wondering if you wanted to hang out."

"Not tonight, thanks," Jenn said.

"What's up?" Julie asked.

Jenn sobbed and tried to stop herself. "I'm just not feeling that great." Jenn started crying again.

"Are you in your dorm?" Julie asked.

"Yes," Jenn said.

"Stay there. I'll be over in fifteen minutes."

"You don't have to-"

"Are you saying you don't want me there?" Julie asked quietly.

Jenn thought for a moment. "No," she said.

"Then I'll be there. Fifteen minutes, okay?"

"Okay," Jenn replied. She hung up. There was something comforting about knowing Julie was coming to see her. It was closer to ten minutes when someone knocked on Jenn's door. Jenn jumped and looked through the peephole. It was Julie.

Jenn opened the door and Julie stepped in to hug her. Julie shut the door behind her and the two of them stood like that while Jenn tried not to cry.

"What happened?" Julie asked, when Jenn finally let her go.

"I went to see Luke," Jenn began.

"If that asshole hurt you-" Julie began.

Jenn waved Julie's objections away. Julie held Jenn's hand and looked at her forearm. "That's not nothing," Julie said.

Jenn nodded. "I've been intimidated by men before, but he's got something more," she said. "There's a power there I didn't know he had." She started shaking.

"Is it okay if I read your mind?" Julie asked, guiding Jenn to sit on her bed.

Jenn nodded. She wasn't going to be able to tell the story coherently anyway. Jenn waited for just a moment until Julie reacted.

"How could he do that to you?" Julie snapped. "I'm going down there right now-" She stopped herself and looked at Jenn. Julie settled herself back on the bed. "No, I'm not," she amended. "I'm staying here with you."

"Thank you," Jenn replied. "When he started glowing he-" She tried to find the right words. "I feel like he was about to lose control and if he did, I wouldn't be here right now."

Julie wrapped her arm around Jenn's shoulders, but Jenn continued shaking. "I'm sorry for what I said before," Julie said.

"What did you say?" Jenn asked.

"I asked if you loved Luke. I'm sorry that I asked it now."

Jenn laughed. "That's not the worst thing that's happened this summer by far."

Julie laughed a little too. "I suppose you're right." She looked around and saw a blanket loose at the end of the bed. She pulled it over hers and Jenn's legs.

"I'm in shock," Jenn stated.

"Yes, you are," Julie agreed, "but it's expected after something like that."

"It's great to be normal," Jenn replied, trying to make a joke.

"What are we going to do?" Julie asked.

"Well, I usually watch a TV show after Luke traumatizes me," Jenn joked.

"I meant long-term. But maybe you're right. This really isn't the time to plan."

"It's really not," Jenn agreed. She stood up long enough to get her laptop and got back on the bed. "If we're going to be watching a show, we'll need to reconfigure," Jenn said. She and Julie ended up sitting at the top of her bed, leaning against the wall, with the laptop on their laps. "Have you seen this one before?" Jenn asked, clicking over to the show she was watching.

"No," Julie said. "I don't watch as much TV as some people."

Jenn laughed. "We'll have to fix that." She clicked to the first episode. "You'll love it."

It was several hours later when Julie said that she needed to get home. "Will you be okay?" Julie asked.

"I think so," Jenn said. "I don't feel like I'm in shock anymore."

"Always a good thing," Julie replied.

"Julie?"

"Yes?"

"Thank you."

Julie smiled. "Of course. You know I'm always here for you."

Jenn smiled. "The same goes for you."

They hugged again and Julie left. Jenn turned out the light and settled back into her bed. She turned the volume down on her laptop, clicked over to the last episode she had watched, and let it play until she fell asleep.

**

Julie checked in with Jenn over text the next few days, but it wasn't until the following week that the two saw each other again.

"I've been thinking," Jenn said, "Luke wanted you to find someone in particular with your magic, right?"

"Probably," Julie said. They had met at the Royal Latte again, but Jenn had given her real name to the barista this time.

"So, what do you want to bet he wanted you to find Huginn and Muginn?"

Julie's eyes widened and she nodded. "That would make sense."

"Let's try to find them first."

"How?" Julie asked.

"Well," Jenn thought. "You said there were other people who felt like Luke around, right?"

"Yes," Julie said cautiously. "There's two kind of near here, it's hard to tell geography when I'm in there. There are others, but they're a long way away and I can't really tell where."

"Luke must have come to this town for a reason, and I doubt it's that bar. The two near here are probably the ones he's looking for."

"Do you think they're actually ravens?" Julie asked.

Jenn shrugged. "A raven is a weird pet, but I suppose I've seen weirder."

"I can try to find them and see what they feel like," Julie said. "Achi and Abe are both magical, but they feel different, you know? One of them flies and the other lives in water."

"I don't know, but go on," Jenn replied.

Julie smiled. "So, I can see if those two minds feel like Achi, or if they feel more like Luke, which would mean they're probably in a human form."

"I think I follow you," Jenn said.

"I'm just making this up as I go," Julie confided.

"That does not fill me with confidence," Jenn replied.

Julie shrugged. "Well, that's all we've got right now, so I'm going to run with it." She closed her eyes and slowed her breathing. Jenn hadn't realized Julie was going to use her magic here and now. Jenn looked around the café, but no one seemed to care about what they were doing. Which was, Jenn had to admit, why they met here. Jenn had been prepared to tell someone they were LARPing if anyone asked, and she was a little disappointed she didn't get to use her speech on anyone.

Jenn watched Julie's face for a change and she was not disappointed. "Found them," Julie said quietly. She kept her eyes closed for another moment, and then opened them again. "They're in human form, I think."

"Great," Jenn said. "That will make this easier. Then we can talk to them and find out why Luke is trying to track them down."

"It's strange, though," Julie said. "There was one human in the house with them and seven who weren't quite human but weren't quite magic."

"Do you think those are their guards?"

"I don't know," Julie said, her face clouding. "They're in human form now, if that helps."

"Not really," Jenn replied. "That makes it ten against two and I don't like our odds."

"But with your silver tongue, we have nothing to fear," Julie told her laughing.

"We might be getting in way over our heads here," Jenn said.

"I didn't expect caution from you," Julie replied.

"But," Jenn continued, "if we don't go, then Luke might get there first and we'll never know why he wanted them. I think it will be better for Huginn and Muninn if we get there first."

"That's what I was expecting," Julie said. "Let's run in there and fake it."

Jenn shrugged. "It's worked for me so far."

"If we get into trouble, you can always call Luke," Julie said.

Jenn glared at her.

"So that he can be a distraction while we leave," Julie finished. "I thought you'd be fine with putting him in harm's way."

"That part I'm fine with. I just do not want to call him."

"Fair," Julie replied. "Then I can. He gave me his card too."

"Of course he did," Jenn said. "Well, shall we rush in?"

"Of course," Julie replied, standing up.

They left Royal Latte and went to Jenn's car. "Hang on a sec," Jenn said, opening the trunk. She dug through a lot of stuff, but eventually came up with two clipboards. They both had paper on them and Jenn found two pens a moment later.

"Why clipboards?" Julie asked.

"Because they make you look official," Jenn answered. "You can get in anywhere with a clipboard if you pretend like you're supposed to be there."

"Did you just give me a trade secret?" Julie asked in mock wonder.

"It's because I like you," Jenn said, getting into her car.

"I'll try not to swoon," Julie said, getting in and buckling her seat belt.

Jenn laughed and left the parking lot. "You know how to get there, right?"

"Mostly," Julie said. She pulled out her phone and opened up the maps app. "It was over here," she said.

Jenn just drove until Julie gave her directions. She glanced over and noticed Julie's eyes were closed.

Suddenly, Julie's phone said, "Recalculating. Turn right on Wright St."

"Did you just magic your GPS?" Jenn asked, turning right.

"I think so?" Julie asked, staring at her phone.

"I think that makes you a technopagan," Jenn said.

"A what?" Julie asked.

"Although I'm not sure if that refers to the music or technology." Jenn kept a straight face for a moment, and then laughed.

"Why do I even bother?" Julie asked.

"Because I'm hilarious," Jenn replied, making another turn. "This place isn't too far away, right?"

"We'll be there in ten minutes," Julie said, looking at her phone.

"Not far at all," Julie said. "Kind of funny they were so close to us the whole time."

"Well, you typically can't ask someone if they used to be a raven working for a Norse god."

"That's a pity," Jenn answered.

In about ten minutes, they pulled up to the house Julie's phone had guided them to. Jenn parked across the street.

"Well," Julie said. "What's the plan?"

Jenn looked the house over and noticed a car in the driveway. "Looks like they went to the same high school we did," she said, looking at the bumper sticker for an honor student at Melodia High School.

"How old do you think they are?" Julie asked.

Jenn shrugged. "Doesn't matter. We're doing a survey for the high school. If they graduated, we're talking to alums. If they're still there, we're talking to current students."

"And how will you tell?" Julie asked.

"People tell you a lot if you ask them the right questions," Jenn said. "Come on. Let's go."

They got out of the car and walked across the street. Jenn confidently rang the doorbell. She turned around to tell Julie to let her do the talking and was face to face with Luke. She flinched backward. "What the hell are you doing here?" she whispered.

"Not ruining your con," Luke said. "I can play along."

The door opened and Jenn spun around, putting on a smile. "Hello," she said. "We're here doing a survey for Melodia High School."

"The high school? What about?" the girl asked. Jenn decided to take a gamble. "We're looking to ask alumni a few questions."

"Just alumni?" the girl asked, looking annoyed. Obviously, she still went there and found it as annoying as just about any other high school kid.

"Yes," Jenn told her. "There will be another survey for current students later."

"Okay," the girl replied, shrugging. She turned around and yelled up the stairs, "Boys! You've got visitors!" She turned back to Jenn, Julie, and Luke. "This way," she said, leading them into a living room.

As they sat down, Jenn could hear what sounded like a small herd of elephants clumping down the stairs and into the living room. Then again, it was nine teenage boys, so it wasn't that far off. They all looked like they had different parents, and Jenn wondered if this was a foster home.

"Hello," Jenn said. "We're from Melodia High School and we're doing a survey about your time there to try to improve it. Before we begin, do you have any questions?"

"Did you go there too?" one of the boys asked. Some of his hair was dyed purple.

"Yes," Jenn said and Julie nodded.

"What about him?" another boy asked. He was wearing a red flannel shirt.

"He's our trainee," Jenn said. "He's never really done surveys before."

"I'm here to learn," Luke said happily.

"So," Jenn said. "Let's start with what you didn't like."

Predictably, the boys complained about some of the teachers, the preferential treatment that sports got over everything else, and the food in the cafeteria. One of the boys complained about the five-paragraph essay. "I never use it in college," he said. "My professor told us to forget about it."

"I know what you mean," Jenn replied, writing everything down. Eventually, she had to stop the boys from talking or they would be there all night. "If you think of anything else, just write it down and mail it to the survey department at the high school," Jenn said with a smile.

"Sure," the purple haired boy said. "I'm sure we'll think of something else."

"Have a nice night," Jenn said with a smile and the door closed behind them. Jenn turned to Luke, her smile in place. "Take a walk with me," she commanded.

"Of course, my dear," Luke said. "We have much to discuss."

Jenn, Julie, and Luke walked around the corner. Once she was sure the boys couldn't see them anymore, Jenn stopped and turned to face Luke with Julie standing next to her.

"What the actual Hell was that?" Jenn snapped.

Luke put up his hands defensively. "I was trying to track you down to apologize. I thought you were going to a friend's house."

"So, you're still stalking me and trying to stop me from seeing my friends. That's abusive behavior, you know. Besides the obvious, I mean."

"That's part of what I wanted to apologize for. I had…a very hard life when I lived with my family. There were many things that made me leave and one of them was how violent they were to me. When you slapped me the other night, it…brought some things back. I'm not saying what I did was right. I know that it wasn't. I was just acting on instinct."

"Even if I accepted that apology, which I don't, that still doesn't explain you poking your nose into my family. How did you even find Perdita, anyway?"

"As I told you, I was only trying to help. It was clear you'd had a bad experience with your magic and I just followed your magical signature. Did you know you've impacted a lot of people with your magic?"

"I'm sure I have," Jenn agreed sarcastically.

"Fine," Luke said, dismissing that point. "In any event, I figured out that Perdita was the one most likely to be giving you pause about using your magic again, so I cured her. I didn't think it would be a problem."

"You had to know I'd find out. You called yourself Dr. Luke, for God's sake!"

"Which god?" Luke asked. Then, before Jenn could answer, "I wanted you to know that it worked and I didn't want you worried about someone you didn't know using magic on your cousin. I can tell she means a lot to you."

Julie put a hand on Jenn's shoulder and Jenn realized she'd been balling her hands into fists so tightly she was probably about to hurt herself. Jenn took a breath and tried to calm herself down. "If you thought I'd be worried about someone else using magic on her, did you think that might include you?" Jenn asked as calmly as she could.

Luke sighed. "We've known each other for months now and you still don't trust me?"

"I've reminded you of why I don't trust you several times, but I can tell you again if you need me to," Jenn replied.

"My dear, everything I've done has been to help you. I'm sorry if it came across the wrong way. I even awakened Julie's power for her now so she would have someone to help her through it. Otherwise, it could have happened with no one around to help her and the results could have been dire."

Jenn stared at Luke. "I knew you had something to do this with that!" she spat. "What is wrong with you? Are you trying to make Julie think she's insane?"

"She would have if her powers had come out when I wasn't around to help her."

"If you weren't around?!" Jenn screamed.

"Please stop talking about me like I'm not here," Julie said calmly.

Both Jenn and Luke turned to her, stunned.

"Luke, are you saying that you saw I had these powers and somehow awakened them in me now so you could help me learn how to use them? And the alternative would have been them awakening on their own when I might have just thought I was going crazy?"

Luke cleared his throat. "Yes, that is exactly what I was saying. When I saw that you were friends with Jenn, I knew I had to help you."

"Help her?" Jenn spat.

"Jenn," Julie still managed to sound calm and in control. "Luke had his reasons for his actions. I can't say I would want to go through that without anyone to help me with it. Whether he did the right thing or not is hard to say, but it seems like his intentions were good."

Jenn snorted, but she knew Julie wouldn't want her to keep screaming at Luke.

"Thank you," Luke said to Julie. He turned back to Jenn. "I am sorry for any distress I caused either of you."

Jenn was not done with him yet. "Yeah, well, stalking will do that."

Luke looked at Jenn's arms. There were four purple bruises on the tops of her forearms. Luke held out his hand. Jenn glared at him. Luke looked back at her with the patience of centuries. Rolling her eyes, Jenn put her hand in Luke's. He held her arm up higher and gently turned it over to reveal a fifth purple bruise on the underside.

"May I heal you?" he asked Jenn.

"No," Jenn stated, taking her hand back. "I want to remember what you did to me."

"Luke, you've said what you've come to say," Julie said, stepping forward a little. "I think it's time for you to go."

"Jenn-" Luke began.

Jenn put up her hand. "I really don't want to hear any more of your bullshit. Stop stalking me and just leave me alone."

"Very well," Luke said. He held out his right hand. Again, Jenn knew he was never going to move unless she put her hand in his. Luke gave her a firm handshake. "It's been a pleasure knowing you," he said. "Please come find me if you need me."

"I won't," Jenn said, pulling her hand away and wiping it on her shorts.

Luke nodded sadly. Then he turned and walked away. Jenn waited until he was gone and then she turned back to Julie. "That bastard," Jenn snarled.

"You handled that very well," Julie told her.

Jenn deflated. She was caught off guard by the compliment. "Thank you," she said.

"Of course," Julie replied. "Now, let's get back in your car and talk about what we learned in that house."

Jenn's car was only a short walk away. "I'm going to drive away so they don't get suspicious," Jenn said. "If they aren't already," she added, turning the car on.

"So," Julie said, once they had left that block behind, "The boy with the black glasses and the boy with the red hair were the ones who were different."

"So they're our Huginn and Muninn," Jenn said. "I guess the only good thing about Luke showing up is that we know we're in the right place. Why else would he bother?"

"He was looking for you?" Julie asked carefully.

Jenn waved that aside. "If he can stalk me, he can find me when I'm alone. No, he wanted to be there when we went in. Are we going to talk about how he activated your powers?"

"No," Julie replied. She caught Jenn's look. "It won't do anything right now, although that is something I'm going to have to think about."

"I wonder if he gave you powers so I would come back to him," Jenn said slowly.

"What do you mean?" Julie asked.

"I wasn't planning on ever seeing him again, but I had to once you started reading minds."

"So everything is about you?" Julie joked.

Jenn frowned. "I hope not, but it kind of looks that way." She was quiet for a moment. "If he went messing around in your head just so I would talk to him again, I'll kill him."

"Let's not worry about it for now," Julie suggested. "We've got plenty of other things to worry about besides me. Like why Luke showed up and came into the house with us. I guess it was probably to stop us from saying anything that would give our suspicions away."

"You bet your ass," Jenn replied, deciding she would drop their other conversation for now.

"So, what do we do?" Julie asked.

Jenn was silent for awhile. "We need to get back there to talk to those boys when Luke isn't there."

"When do we go back?" Julie asked. "And what do we say to them? They probably think they're humans."

"You're right," Jenn said. "I guess we can't start prattling on about Norse mythology to them."

"Probably not," Julie agreed. She thought for a moment. "If we're going against Luke, we should bring everything we have."

"Agreed," Jenn said, gripping the steering wheel.

"Don't you think it's time we figured out how your magic works?" Julie asked.

Jenn glanced over at her, and then put her focus back on the road. "How do you think we can do that? I don't even know how it happens."

"Do you remember what happened between you and Perdita?" Julie asked gently.

Jenn thought. "We were at the top of the zipline and she said she didn't want to be afraid of heights anymore. Then something passed between us and she wasn't."

"That's it?" Julie asked. "She just said she didn't want to and she wasn't?"

"I don't remember exactly what she said," Jenn replied.

"I could read your mind and find out," Julie told her.

Jenn sighed. "You just love getting into my head, don't you?" She smiled a little at Julie. "It's the best lead we've got, I guess," she said. Jenn pulled over into the parking lane and put the car in park.

"Right now?" Julie asked.

"No time like the present," Jenn replied, shrugging.

Julie closed her eyes and Jenn could see her face focusing. For her part, Jenn tried to remember that day and the drive out to her cousins' house. The missing purple hair clip. How they all went out to the obstacle course. Jenn being so slow at it. Standing at the top with Perdita. Suddenly, Jenn was there.

They were at the top with the zip line. George clipped his harness onto one of the lanyards at the top of the course, pushed off, and rocketed down the line, yelling all the way.

Reina went next, followed by Donna. Then it was just Jenn and Perdita. "I'm not sure I want to do this," Perdita said, grabbing Jenn's hand.

"Why not?" Jenn asked.

"Mom and Dad have always been here before, and this is really tall." Perdita looked down at the ground. *"I wish I wasn't afraid of heights."*

Jenn felt something on her hand, almost like getting shocked by static electricity, and Perdita started smiling. Perdita let go of Jenn's hand, clipped her harness onto the line, and shot down the zipline almost as fast as George had.

Jenn blinked back to the here and now and saw Julie looking at her. "You granted her wish," Julie said.

"I suppose I did," Jenn replied. She laughed. "Maybe I'm her fairy godmother."

"Do you always grant people's wishes?" Julie asked.

Jenn shrugged. "People always get what they wish for in the worst way, but I don't know if that's me or the world."

"Hm." Julie looked around. "I wish I had a latte right now."

Nothing happened.

"See?" Jenn asked. "Let's stop worrying about my magic and focus on how we're going to kick Luke's ass."

Julie grabbed Jenn's arm. "I wish I had a latte right now."

"I don't know why you're still trying this," Jenn said. She had felt something when Julie grabbed her arm, but it was probably nothing. Julie was silent. Jenn looked over and saw a latte in Julie's other hand. Julie set it in the cupholder carefully. Jenn poked it. It seemed solid enough. She took off the lid. There was a latte inside, but it was cold and had started to grow mold. "Ew," Jenn said.

"Gross," Julie replied.

Jenn put the lid back on it.

"I guess that was a pretty bad way to get a latte," Julie said, looking at it sideways.

"I guess," Jenn said. She looked up at Julie. "So, I grant wishes, then?"

"I guess so," Julie replied, "but I don't think I want to make another wish. Do you remember that story…oh what was it called? This old couple got a magical thing that gave them three wishes and the first one they used for money and they got that exact amount, but only because their son died at work. One night, the wife used the second wish to bring him back from the dead."

"And the husband used the third wish to put him back," Jenn finished. "I remember that story. 'The Monkey's Paw' I think."

"That's right," Julie replied. "It's kind of like that."

"I don't think I've killed anyone!" Jenn replied.

"I don't think so either," Julie replied too quickly. "I just think it works like that. You have to be really specific to get what you want."

"Can you throw that latte out?" Jenn asked.

"Sure," Julie replied. Fortunately, Jenn had parked close to a garbage can, so Julie was back in the car quickly. Jenn pulled away from the curb and started driving. "I guess I can't let people touch me when they make a wish," Jenn said after a moment.

"Probably for the best," Julie replied.

"Unless I want something bad to happen to them," Jenn continued. "Like Luke. Maybe I should try to get him to wish for something stupid. He always seems to be touching me anyway."

"That would mean you have to see him again," Julie replied.

"True," Jenn agreed. "True, and I really don't want to do that." They were quiet for the rest of the drive.

"I'm so glad I have a late day tomorrow," Julie said. "I'm exhausted."

"I guess you did use your magic a lot today," Jenn realized.

Julie gave her a small smile. "That's okay. It'll help me grow."

"Maybe," Jenn replied.

Julie rolled her eyes. "We'll say it will. I'll text you if I think of any way to convince those boys they're ravens."

"Same," Jenn replied laughing. Julie got out of the car and Jenn waited for her to get inside her house before she drove away.

It was frustrating to be so close to the answer and not know what it was. She would love to get Luke to tell her, but she shied away from that thought. She truly did not want to see him again and especially not alone. Jenn wondered how long it would be until she could start wearing long sleeves to cover up her bruises. Maybe she should wear a ton of bracelets until then. Jenn mused on this until she got back to her parking spot and headed into her dorm. She had a class to go to soon, which at least gave her something to do.

**

"We've got to go back to that house today," Jenn texted Julie the next day. "Luke moves fast and we want to beat him."

"True. When?" Julie texted back.

"3?" Jenn asked.

"Sure," Julie replied.

Jenn managed to make it through her classes and the time to go came along sooner than she thought it would. She ran to her car to go pick up Julie.

"So, what's the plan?" Julie asked as Jenn drove back to the boys' house.

"Gut Luke if he shows up," Jenn replied.

Julie sighed. "Anything else?"

"Well, I suppose we could wish for them to remember who they used to be," Jenn said after a moment.

"Aren't you worried what would happen to them?" Julie asked.

"Of course I am," Jenn replied. She realized she was gripping the steering wheel too hard. "I'm really hesitant about using my magic when I don't really understand it yet, but it's the only idea I've got."

Julie considered. "I've been thinking about this since yesterday and I can't think of a better plan, either. Besides trying to kidnap them."

"That would be a terrible idea," Jenn replied.

"Yes, it would," Julie agreed. "So, what, do we show up and ask to talk to just those two?"

"We could make the wish on them from the car," Jenn replied, "and then run into the house after it's done."

"How will we know when it's done?"

"When we see two ravens flying out the window," Jenn joked. She considered for a moment. "It seems to be pretty quick. I don't think we'd really have to wait at all."

"So, we get there, make the wish, and run in?" Julie asked.

"That's pretty much my plan," Jenn agreed. They were getting close to the house. Jenn tried to think of how to word the wish so it went exactly as they wanted. Soon enough, they came to the house and parked across the street.

"Jenn, they're not there," Julie said quietly.

"What?" Jenn asked, unbuckling her seatbelt.

"Maybe they've got class," Julie said.

"That bastard beat us," Jenn said, looking at the house where the front door stood open. In a moment, she was out of the car and running up to the house. The girl who lived there came out to meet her.

"Are you here to take the rest of my brothers?!" she yelled.

"What do you mean?" Julie asked, behind Jenn.

"That man who was here with you before. He came here and asked to see my brothers again for the survey. Then he…he…turned two of them into ravens." The girl looked disoriented and she started to fall. Jenn caught her, then quickly put her on the ground, leaning against the house, and stepped back. She did not want to grant this girl's wishes.

"We believe you," Julie told the girl.

The girl nodded distractedly. "I've seen that before. Before now. The rest of my brothers. All seven turned to ravens." She put her hand up to pull her hair away from her face and Jenn noticed the girl was missing a pinky, but that seemed to have happened long ago.

Jenn began to get worried this girl had gotten a concussion.

"I was so young when it happened, but I went out to save them," the girl began. "I went to the sun, but he was so scary. I went to the moon, but she was no help. I went to the stars…" Her face relaxed and she stopped speaking for a moment. "…they were lovely," she continued. "They gave me a drumstick to open the door in the mountain with. When I got there, the drumstick was gone."

"Just like Luke," Jenn growled, but Julie hushed her.

"But I had to open the lock," the girl continued like she hadn't been interrupted. "All I had was my pinky," she held up her hand and stared at it. "My pinky finger. It fit in the lock so well and turned, but then it wouldn't come back out." The girl shivered. "So I left it there. Inside, I found their meal and I took a little from each plate. I left our mother's engagement ring in their cup so they would know it was me. When they came back, all seven became human again and we went home, but there were nine now. Nine brothers." The girl, confused, looked up at Julie. "How did I get two more brothers?"

"The man who was with us yesterday brought them to you then," Julie said.

"He was trying to hide them and he found them again," Jenn said. "That bastard."

"But they're my brothers," the girl protested.

"Where are the rest of your brothers?" Jenn asked.

"Inside," the girl told her. "They've become ravens again, but my mother has her engagement ring, so I don't know what I am to do."

Jenn looked at Julie. They both stood up and went inside. The boys had draped themselves across the furniture as humans; as ravens, they stood almost at attention. It was eerie having seven ravens staring you down in complete silence inside a house.

"What do we do?" Jenn asked quietly.

Julie was silent for a moment. "They've done this before," she began slowly, "maybe if I can remind them how they changed back the first time…"

"And how will you do that?" Jenn asked.

Julie turned, slowly, to face her. "I'll have to read their minds and pull up the right memory."

"You'll have to what?" Jenn asked, incredulous. "You've never done that before."

"I know," Julie replied, "but what else can we do?"

"Go after the other two," Jenn replied. "You can bet Luke's got them, and I bet they're in his cave right now."

"We can't leave them," Julie scolded her, "and this plan is a lot better than trying to wish them human again." For a moment, Jenn and Julie stared each other down.

Jenn sighed. "Fine, but if your plan doesn't work, we're leaving."

"All right," Julie agreed. She slowly sat down and leaned against the wall. She closed her eyes and started breathing more slowly and deeply. Jenn stared down the ravens. If any of them tried to move against Julie, they'd have to deal with her.

For several long moments, nothing happened. Jenn became more and more unnerved by the constant stares of the birds. Then, as one, their heads twitched to the side. It looked like a motion birds did frequently, but Jenn had never seen seven ravens do it at once together. Their heads twitched the other way. Their beaks all opened, but nothing came out. Jenn edged toward Julie but didn't touch her just in case Julie was the one doing this. From outside, the girl picked herself up and limped into the living room.

"My brothers," she murmured.

Julie inhaled sharply. Then, all at once, the air was full of swirling feathers and a bright light. When Jenn was able to see again, there were no more ravens in the room. There weren't even any feathers. There were just seven confused teenage boys and one teenage girl crying and trying to hug them all at once.

"My brothers!" she said, turning to Jenn and Julie. "You brought them back!"

"Of course we did," Jenn replied, helping Julie stand up and head to the door.

"Where are you going?" the girl asked.

"To get the other two," Julie replied over her shoulder. Jenn had to help her walk to the car and Julie settled herself into the car seat with a sigh.

"Are you okay?" Jenn asked.

Julie shook her head. "I'm drained," she replied. "I didn't realize it would be that hard."

"I did try to warn you," Jenn said, driving away.

"This is not the time for I told you so," Julie replied.

"I know," Jenn said, looking at the road. "How do you think we'll get into the Velvet Tango Lounge?"

"Do you think he'd take them back there?" Julie asked.

"Well, he certainly didn't hide what he did here. I think he wants us to come and find him, so he'll probably be exactly where we expect him to be."

"Why do you think he wants us to find him?" Julie asked.

"As soon as I met Luke, I knew he was the kind of person who uses people," Jenn began. "He's got a plan for every interaction to either make him better off, or to trick the other person. Every. Interaction."

"Except with you," Julie told her.

Jenn nodded. "What's so damn special about me?" she asked. "He wants to use me for something big."

"Or maybe, in his twisted, abusive way, he's in love with you," Julie replied.

"It could be both!" Jenn snapped. She sighed. "God, I hope it's not both."

"He's certainly been trying," Julie said.

Jenn shook her head. "Either way. He told me I had magic within five minutes of meeting me. Accused me of it, really. He keeps saying I'm powerful and that he wants to train me how to use my power."

"You're part of his plan," Julie realized.

Jenn nodded. "I'm not sure what he wants me to do, but you can bet he wants it to happen now."

"So we're playing into his hands?" Julie asked.

Jenn shrugged. "I'd rather go meet him on my terms rather than have him follow me."

"…or have him hurt me to get to you," Julie added softly.

A muscle jumped in Jenn's jaw. "I don't think he's above that," she said at last.

"So having me with you will make me safer?" Julie asked.

"Maybe," Jenn said. "I can try to protect you." As an afterthought, she said, "And you can have my mace."

"You did use it on him before," Julie agreed. "What about you?" Julie asked.

"He won't hurt me," Jenn said.

"You mean like he's already done?" Julie asked.

"He's more likely to hurt you," Jenn amended. "With me, it's an accident. With you, it could be a plan."

Julie nodded, but her lips were in a thin line.

Jenn slid into a parking space and shot out of the car. She waited for Julie at the top of the stairs to the Velvet Tango Lounge and handed Julie her can of mace. "So, are we breaking in?" Julie asked.

"Maybe," Jenn replied. They made their way down the stairs. Jenn tried the door and it opened under her hand. She took a deep breath. She would have to try not to lose her temper at Luke. That would only make things worse. She took another breath. Julie's hand slid into hers and Jenn gave it a squeeze. The two of them walked in together.

The lights were on, but the sunlight coming in through the few windows was brighter.

"Good afternoon, ladies," Luke said from the bar. "I've been waiting for you." He saluted them with his glass and drank from it.

"What does one drink after turning nine boys into ravens?" Jenn asked icily.

Luke shrugged. "It was easier to turn them all at once since they'd been turned into humans together."

"Was it really?" Jenn asked, standing in front of him.

Luke shrugged and tilted his glass a little. "It brought you back to me," he replied.

"I am here to find out what you think you're playing at," Jenn told him.

"Simply righting a wrong," Luke said.

"A wrong that you caused," Jenn snapped.

Julie put a hand on Jenn's shoulder. "What happened with them?" she asked Luke.

"It was a typical story of a sister saving her fowl brothers," Luke said with a shrug. "I saw an opening and I took it."

"So, you managed to kidnap Huginn and Muninn and turn them into humans?" Jenn asked incredulously. "Was Odin mad?" she taunted.

"Oh, he was as angry as I've ever seen him," Luke replied with a laugh. "My brother was always one to overreact."

"Your brother?" Jenn asked, her mind whizzing with that she knew of Norse mythology. "Odin?"

"Oh yes," Luke replied. "I was wondering if you would figure this part out or not." He smiled a dazzling smile at Julie. "My apologies." Then, all at once, he was glowing again. His hair became a dark, glowing black and he lit up the room. It was like the night Jenn had slapped him, but this was even stronger. It would have been beautiful, except that his face was horribly scarred and there were small circular scars above and below his lips. Like his mouth had once been sewn shut.

"Loki?!" Jenn yelled.

"At your service, my dear," Luke replied with a bow.

Jenn looked at Julie to see her reaction, but she had crumpled to the ground. "Julie!" Jenn bent down to try to help her friend.

"Don't worry about her," Luke commanded. "Mortals can't handle the full manifestation of a god."

"Mortals?" Jenn asked, standing up. "Then what am I?"

"An interesting puzzle," Luke replied with a grin. "I knew from the start that you were a half-breed of some sort, but I couldn't tell what."

"Half white, half Chinese," Jenn snapped.

"That's not what I meant," Luke replied gently. "Part of you was human, but part of you was so much more. You had a level of magic I've rarely seen. I asked Abe if he could tell, but he was little help. It wasn't until I realized that you were granting wishes that I realized what you were."

"A fairy godmother?" Jenn asked sarcastically.

Luke laughed. "Oh goodness no. You're half djinn, my dear."

"Djinn?" Jenn asked. "Don't you mean genie?"

Luke looked at her for a moment, and then laughed a little. "So you don't know. My dear, a genie is the tamed version of what was never meant to be tamed. Djinns live to cause discord and mayhem. They were all trapped in bottles and made to grant wishes, but the third wish always had to be to put the djinn back in the bottle, or they would be free again."

Jenn felt her back prickling. "So, I'm a monster," she said.

"Not at all," Luke said, standing. "You're wonderful."

Jenn took a step back.

"I have a proposition for you, my dear," Luke said.

"Not interested," Jenn snapped.

"Poor choice of words," Luke replied apologetically, but with a glint in his eye. "I am trying to make a world for those with magic."

"Excuse me?" Jenn asked.

"For far too long, we've been relegated to the shadows," Luke told her. "Hiding our skills, terrified that a human without magic would find us. It has to end and I know how to end it."

"I'll just bet you do," Jenn muttered.

"The other gods don't see this the way I do," Luke told her. "Odin, greedy as he is, wants all magic to be kept to the gods and to be kept hidden so humans don't surpass him."

"Aren't you worried about that?" Jenn asked.

Luke grinned. "I welcome the challenge."

Jenn was having trouble wrapping her mind around all of this. "So, you stole Huginn and Muninn from Odin and hid them with a human family. Then, I'm assuming you forgot about them while you raised a magical army. Eventually, Odin realized you had to be the one who kidnapped them, so he charged you with finding them, but your army wasn't ready yet." The pieces fell into place for Jenn. "You had to be powerful to defeat the gods without an army, and I haven't seen a giant anywhere. So, you needed someone with power to rival a god who would change the world with you." Jenn tried to keep the anger out of her voice. "You needed me."

"Right on the nose," Luke replied with a grin. "It all fits together when you see the bigger picture, doesn't it? Our goals are the same, my dear. We both want to create a world where Julie can be who she is without having to worry about being labelled insane. A world where you can be who you are without having to worry any time someone touches you." He reached out and traced the edge of Jenn's cheek. Jenn snapped her face away. Luke smiled at her. "Your magic only works for mortals. Even if we are touching, you're unable to grant a wish for me."

Jenn remembered Luke trying this. He had wished that she would trust him. A bad feeling began in Jenn's gut, but she did her best to hide it. "I guess we have to keep it even," Jenn replied flatly.

"It's part of Solomon's seal," Luke replied, as if this were a detail. "Later, we can remove the seal entirely, but things are moving too fast now to attempt that."

"Of course they are," Jenn thought. "What things?" she asked.

"Now that I've found Huginn and Muninn, Odin won't be far behind," Luke told her. "We need to act when he's here on Midgard."

"We?" Jenn asked.

"Yes," Luke replied, stepping slowly toward her. "Together, you and I can remake this world so no one has to hide in the shadows again. Together, we can defeat the gods and give Julie a world where she won't be treated as different. Achi can fly in the sun again. Abe can swim where he likes and teach anyone. And you…" Luke placed his hands on Jenn's shoulders, "you can be whatever you wish to be. You've felt the battle between your two halves your whole life. Wouldn't it be nice to set that aside and just be one Jenn and leave aside the loneliness that difference causes? In this new world, there's no more feeling alone in a crowd, or counting your friends on one hand. You can finally feel like you belong."

Jenn took a deep, shaking breath. It was like he knew her secret wishes. He spoke to exactly what appealed to her. She was so tired of feeling alone when she was with her friends.

"Jenn," Luke said, drawing her gaze to his face instantly, "help me make this a reality for you and for everyone. Julie could use her mind-reading to be a better social worker and not have to lie about it. You could make magic happen for businesses and negotiate the best contract for everyone involved, but the best by far for you. Think about it. You have to choose to be human or djinn. Free your djinn-self and make this new world a reality for Julie."

His eyes were almost hypnotic and Jenn felt herself falling into his words. Gradually, she could feel the two halves of herself: human and djinn. The two had learned to coexist but had never thrived together because she had never acknowledged half of herself. It was strange that she had never noticed it before. Jenn took a deep breath. No more battling. She could choose one or the other and she could make this world into whatever she wanted it to be.

"My dear," Luke said gently. "What kind of a world would it be without magic?"

Suddenly, Jenn reached a decision and she felt the two halves of her shift accordingly. No longer was she split into two. Now she was one. Unified, and it must have shown on her face when she opened her eyes.

Luke grinned widely. "I've been waiting for this moment since the night we met," he told her. "I wanted you to come into your full power, and you have blossomed."

Jenn smiled. "I feel different," she admitted. Her voice sounded different.

Luke nodded. "That is often the case."

"Stronger," Jenn continued. She looked at Luke. "So, what's the plan?"

Luke smiled, leaned forward, and kissed her on the forehead. "Let me lay it out for you." As he explained the plan, his glow gradually dimmed, until he looked human by the end of it. Jenn looked at him again. His hair was neatly combed down a part, with the longer side carefully held in place with product. Jenn wondered if she would feel it if she ran her fingers through his hair. His beard, although blond, was just dark enough to stand out on his face and gave him an air of masculinity and suavity. He was quite the man.

Behind Jenn, Julie was picking herself up off the floor. "What happened?" Julie asked.

"You were tired," Jenn told her. "You fainted."

"You look different," Julie said, looking up at Jenn's face.

Jenn smiled at her. "I know." She helped Julie stand up. "Luke has a plan."

"Really?" Julie asked, her eyebrows going up.

"Really," Jenn replied, a bit firmly.

"Ladies, if we could continue this discussion in the cave?" Luke asked. "My honored guest will be showing up in the few minutes, and we need to be in place when he gets here."

"Honored guest?" Julie asked.

"Odin," Jenn replied shortly.

Julie's eyes went wide. Then three of them walked into Luke's cave. "What's going on?" Julie hissed as they fell behind Luke.

"A lot," Jenn replied shortly. "Luke wants to make a new world."

Julie stopped. "A new what?" she asked.

Jenn grabbed Julie's arm and pulled her up near Luke. Luke opened the door to his bedroom and ushered them both inside. He turned to Julie. "We're going to be changing this world for the better, making it more inclusive, but I need your help. Jenn has the magic, but she needs someone to make a wish to be able to use it."

"You know about that?" Julie asked.

Luke smiled. "I know a lot about Jenn, but I don't have time to get into everything now. I just need you to trust me." He looked at Julie's face. "OK, then trust Jenn. We're going to be going somewhere else. A different world. When we get there, I need you to make a wish so Jenn can grant it."

"What wish?" Julie asked uncertainly.

"I wish that Luke will defeat the gods now to make his new world a reality," Luke recited for her. Jenn could tell he had taken some time to make sure this wish went the way he wanted it to.

"You want to defeat gods?" Julie asked. "What are you talking about?"

"How much do you know about Norse legends?" Luke asked.

"A bit," Julie said.

"Well, they're real. Odin is coming here right now and we need to act while he's still here. We have to go to Asgard to make the wish so he can't interfere and to give Jenn's magic the best chance of working."

"Asgard? The realm of the gods?" Julie asked.

"Don't worry about the specifics," Jenn told her. "Just trust me. We're going to come out of this a whole lot better off."

Julie looked at Jenn for a moment and Jenn wondered if Julie was trying to read her mind. Then, Julie nodded.

"Excellent," Luke said with a smile. "Let me just take us all to the prairie. Odin will be providing our transport." Both girls set their purses down, although Jenn noticed Julie put the mace in her pocket. Luke wrapped an arm around each girl's waist and floated up through the hole in his wall. Then he whizzed down the tunnel and out the top and they were in the prairie.

"How does that work?" Julie asked, staggering a little once Luke set them down.

"Magic, of course," Luke replied with a smile. "Now, we'd better hide."

The three of them crouched in the tall grass and Jenn could feel something resting on them. It almost felt like a blanket, but there was nothing there.

On the path just outside of the hole leading to Luke's caves, there suddenly appeared a man on a horse. Jenn could tell the man was a god because he had the same glow Luke had earlier. That and Julie had passed out again. Jenn looked a bit closer. The man had white, long hair, a lumberjack beard and a black eyepatch. That had to be Odin. Then Jenn looked at the horse. She blinked and counted again. The horse had eight legs. Odin dismounted, looked down at the hole in the ground, sighed, and stepped out over it. Instead of falling, he floated down.

Eventually, he got far enough away that Julie began to revive.

"How do you know we can ride his horse?" Jenn asked Luke, as they crept out of the grass.

"That horse is my son," Luke replied. He walked up to the horse openly. "Sleipnir," he greeted it. "My friends and I need a ride to Asgard."

Sleipnir put his head down and pawed the ground a little bit.

"You know you can't deny me this request," Luke said with a smile.

Sleipnir looked up and whickered at Luke.

"Thank you," Luke replied, smiling.

Perhaps it was because the horse had something to do with the gods, but Julie wasn't back to her normal self. Luke slung her up on Sleipnir's back and slid in behind her, wrapping his arms around her waist. Jenn managed to mount on the back of the horse and wrapped her arms around Luke's waist so she wouldn't fall off. She was surprised that all three of them fit on this horse, but if it was Odin's horse, anything was possible.

The horse began to walk and the scenery around them changed. Sleipnir was galloping on something wooden. It curved a bit away from them on both sides. As they galloped, Sleipnir dodged what looked like a tall tree growing out of the wood. That couldn't be right. Jenn's eyes opened wide as she realized they were riding up the world tree, Yggdrasil. They were really going to Asgard. But how did this work? Were they in space? But there seemed to be plenty of air to breathe. Just before Jenn was going to ask Luke, Sleipnir slowed and stopped. They were now standing in a field outside of a gigantic wall. Jenn looked to the right and to the left, but it stretched as far as she could see in either direction.

Luke slid off of Sleipnir and pulled Julie with him. Jenn slid off behind them and followed as Luke walked Julie some distance from Sleipnir. Eventually, Julie seemed to revive.

"Where are we?" she asked, looking around.

"Asgard," Jenn replied. "If you want to know what's going on, it'll be a lot faster if you just read my mind."

Julie looked at Jenn for a moment, and Jenn could feel Julie in her mind. Then Julie nodded and swayed a little. Jenn hoped the effort wasn't too much for her.

"Do you see why it's so important?" Luke asked. "Think of all the people you could help."

Julie nodded and smiled. Jenn stepped forward and grabbed Julie's hand.

"I wish," Julie began. Jenn squeezed her hand. "I wish Loki would forget everything about his plan to take over the world and that he would stop trying."

With a scream of rage, Luke launched himself at Julie. Jenn stepped between them and grabbed Luke. Julie fell to the ground behind them, and Jenn did her best to drag Luke away. Jenn could feel the power trying to flow through her into Luke but something was stopping it.

"You bitch!" Luke yelled. "I should have found your bottle and stuffed you back inside! I could have found a way to make you obey me."

Jenn gritted her teeth and concentrated on pouring her new-found power into Julie's wish. Now that she had decided to embrace both her djinn-self and her human-self and let them meld together, her power flowed so much more easily.

"You think you know rage, Jenn? You think you know helplessness? I caused the end of the world because of what the gods did to me. I'll do something far worse to you!"

Jenn grabbed onto him harder and tried to ignore his words. She knew she was screwed if this didn't work. His threats didn't mean anything.

"Not just to you," Luke yelled. "I'll come after Julie, and your family. Little Perdita…Your mother."

Jenn screamed and pushed him down. She was still hanging on, so she landed on top of him, knocking the wind out of him for a moment. She closed her eyes and became the wish. It had to be granted, it was part of the law of her seal, and it was Jenn's will. She could feel Luke fighting her, moving this way and take to try to dislodge her. Jenn's fingers dug in until she cut through Luke's skin, but she wouldn't let go. Finally, it was too much, Jenn's power forced its way through and it poured into Luke.

The wish filled up every nook and cranny inside of him. She pushed everything she had into him, to make him forget. She had to make him forget.

Someone was trying to pull her away, but Jenn shook them off and clung onto Luke. Then, a large force ripped her off of him. Dazed, Jenn looked up to find herself confronted by Odin. He was in a fearsome rage.

"What is the meaning of this?" Odin demanded, shaking them both.

Luke smiled. "I'm sure this lovely lady would like to explain," he said. His face went sour. "Because I have no idea who she is." Frowning, Luke massaged his arms and stared as his hand came away with blood on it.

"Luke, I mean, Loki was trying to kill all of you. Again," Jenn said.

Odin glared at her for a moment and Jenn looked him in the eye. After a moment, Odin sighed and set Jenn on the ground. Jenn staggered and almost fell over. She hadn't realized she'd used up that much of her strength.

"He hasn't forgiven you for what happened before the world ended last time," Jenn said. "He was going to use me to defeat all of you again, to make the world into what he wanted." Jenn shivered, remembering how close she'd come to believing him. To believing that he would take that much power and only do good with it.

"He thought you could defeat all of us?" Odin asked. There was no judgement, just a simple question.

Jenn nodded. "I am a djinn," she said. "Well, a djinn and a human."

"Is that why you're able to speak to gods?" Loki asked.

Jenn ignored him and looked at Odin. "I made him forget everything, but the longer we stand here talking, the more he might remember."

Odin nodded, and tossed Loki over to a man wielding a hammer. That must have been Thor. "Take care of him," Odin admonished.

"Just don't do what you did last time," Jenn said, finally letting herself drop to the ground. "It's like after World War I and how they punished Germany. That just made Germany start World War II." She was so tired. She couldn't make a better case, but she needed to make sure they understood her. "He's forgotten it all anyway. Just keep an eye on him and know you can't trust him."

Odin crouched down to be closer to her level. "We know we cannot trust him, but we underestimated him. We will not do that again."

Jenn nodded.

"I will return you to Midgard," Odin said, "brave warrior."

"Julie," Jenn said, looking over to where her friend had fallen.

"Her as well," Odin promised. He whistled and Sleipnir came trotting over. Odin tossed both girls on Sleipnir's back and then mounted behind them.

Jenn was barely able to keep herself conscious for the ride down the world tree. Odin dropped them off at the prairie. "Please," Jenn said, "can you take us inside the cave?"

"Why would you want to go back into Loki's domain?" Odin asked.

Jenn wasn't sure how to tell him that her car was across town from where they were and so was her phone. "Please," she said, instead.

Nodding, Odin picked them up and flew them into the cave. He set them both on Luke's bed. "Rest well, warrior," Odin told her. "And may you one day fall in battle, so we can toast you in Valhalla."

"Thanks?" Jenn asked, as Odin flew away. Now that he was gone, Jenn felt bone tired. She began to relax on the bed. Then she felt Julie move next to her.

"What happened?" Julie asked.

"We won," Jenn said, tiredly. "We're safe."

"You look awful," Julie said.

"Thanks," Jenn replied. Her eyelids were so heavy. She felt Julie curling up next to her, and then Jenn fell asleep.

**

When Jenn woke up, Julie was gone and the bedroom door was standing open. For a moment, Jenn couldn't remember what had happened. She realized she was in Luke's bedroom and began to panic. Then she remembered why she was there and that he had now forgotten everything, including her. She sighed and relaxed. Jenn stretched and began to get up from the bed, grabbing her phone out of her purse. There was one place she had to go before she went to find Julie.

As it turned out, after Jenn left the bathroom, she found Julie in the hallway. "I'm glad you're awake," Julie said. "I've already called off from the diner, but I was going to have to call your mom and tell her not to worry."

"How long did we sleep?" Jenn asked.

"Well, it was Friday afternoon when we went to the boys' house, and now it's Saturday afternoon. I'm not sure how long we were in Asgard but... We slept for a long time."

Jenn stared at her. "The longest I've slept before was twelve hours. This is a new record for me."

"That's what you think of?" Julie asked.

Jenn shrugged.

"Oh, I texted my parents and told them I fell asleep in your dorm room." Julie blushed.

"Okay," Jenn said. "They won't ask my roommate, so that should be fine." She yawned and stretched. "Is there anything to eat in here?" Jenn asked. "I'm starved."

"Not at the bar," Julie replied. "They've just got drinks, but I was looking through the junk room, and I don't think it's junk."

"Sure," Jenn replied, following Julie. "It's antique."

Julie shook her head. She opened the door to the junk room and led Jenn over to a small, low table. Taped to it was a piece of paper that said, "Table be set."

"Table be set?" Jenn asked.

Instantly, a tablecloth appeared on the table and all sorts of food until the little table was groaning under the weight.

Jenn and Julie looked at each other.

"It might be poisoned," Julie began.

"Then I'll eat something and we'll see what happens to me," Jenn said, grabbing a roll from the table and eating it before Julie could object. "I'm half djinn," Jenn said, around the bread roll.

"Looks to me like you're a pig," Julie replied.

Jenn grinned and swallowed her food. Then she sat down and waited. After five minutes, she looked up at Julie. "It's probably fine," she said.

"I guess," Julie said, looking at the table.

Jenn shrugged, stood up, and began eating. She managed to find an empty plate and some silverware, so she loaded up a plate and began devouring it. After another moment, Julie did the same. No matter how much they ate, the table remained full. Eventually, they stopped eating and put their dishes back on the table.

"I wonder how we tell the food to go away," Julie said.

"Why?" Jenn asked.

"I don't want to waste it. And we don't want to get bugs or anything," Julie said.

They looked back at the table, but it was empty again.

"I guess that takes care of that," Jenn replied. "I wonder what else is in here."

"Should we really be poking around at this stuff?" Julie asked.

"Why not?"

"Well, it's not ours."

"Right of conquest," Jenn replied breezily. She looked at Julie's expression. "OK, well. Luke doesn't remember that any of this is here anymore. It's kind of like we just found this stuff and have no way to give it back to its owner. Besides, someone needs to make sure whatever magical creatures show up here are taken care of."

"You think so?" Julie asked. "Wouldn't it be better to just let them go?"

"Go where?" Jenn asked, her mind two steps ahead of her. "They came here because they had nowhere else to go-"

"-or because Luke made them think that," Julie interjected.

"Good point," Jenn replied. "Still. They don't think there's anywhere else to be. Are you going to try to take Achi to your house? You know Katrina is going to try to pet her and slice her fingers open."

Julie shivered. "So, we should keep them here?"

"Until they have somewhere else they want to go. It can be a halfway house."

"A halfway house for magical creatures?" Julie asked. "That sounds like a bad movie."

"Good thing we're not in a movie," Jenn replied. "What do you think? Social workers do something with halfway houses, right?"

Julie laughed and nodded. "Yes."

"And if we're doing that, then we should know what else is in here. If nothing else, we can get free meals when we're working here."

"Jenn, be honest with me. Did you think of how good this would be for everyone before you started pitching this, or were you trying to convince me so you could take stuff from this room?"

Jenn thought for a moment. "Can't it be both?" she asked.

Julie smacked her and Jenn laughed. "I should have known it's like this to deal with you," Julie said.

"I'm just too great for some people," Jenn replied with false sincerity.

Julie rolled her eyes and started looking at what else was in the room. They found a pile of gold rings in one corner, which looked like real gold to Jenn. There was also a stick in a burlap bag, which confused both of them. They tried not to touch the weapons. They weren't sure what kind of magic might be on them and it would probably be more destructive than some of the other objects. As they were rummaging, Julie suddenly stopped and looked at Jenn.

"The boys! That family," Julie said. "We have to tell them what happened to the other two ravens."

"You mean their brothers?" Jenn asked. She looked at Julie's face. "I suppose we'd better."

They collected their purses and snuck out the door and into the bar. The bartender looked up when they came through the door, and then went back to wiping down the bar. Jenn made sure the door locked behind them.

"Why did you do that?" Julie whispered.

"I'll tell you in a bit," Jenn replied, as they exited the bar. Once they got in Jenn's car, she put the address in her GPS and started driving.

"You were going to tell me about locking that door," Julie prompted.

"Oh, right. I stole Luke's keys."

"You what?" Julie asked.

Jenn grinned. "When we were on Sleipnir, I realized that if our plan worked, we wouldn't want him to find those keys, and if it didn't…" Jenn trailed off and shrugged her shoulders, "then we would have bigger problems."

Julie stared at her for a moment. "Do you think like this all the time?" she asked.

"Mostly. If you want to play a good prank, you've got to take your chance whenever you can and that sort of carries over to everything else I do."

Julie shook her head. "It's a wonder you're still alive."

"And on the honor roll," Jenn added.

"So, did you know what you were doing when you told me to make that other wish?" Julie asked.

Jenn's expression dimmed. "I almost didn't think of that wish. I almost believed him that he wanted to make a world where we could be happy."

Julie was quiet.

"We as in me and you," Jenn said. "Not me and him. Never me and him." She shivered and gripped the wheel a little harder.

Julie put her hand on Jenn's shoulder and gave it a quick squeeze.

"So, I don't overthink all the time. I didn't have a lot of time to think of a wish to stop him and getting the wording right so I would do it right. You shouldn't have to outsmart yourself that much."

"What happened after the wish?" Julie asked.

"Well, Luke put his god-face back on, so you probably passed out," Jenn replied.

"You fought him, didn't you?"

Jenn was quiet for a moment, and then nodded. "I've never had to work that hard to grant a wish before, but I couldn't fail. I couldn't let him win…" She cleared her throat. "Odin ended up breaking us up."

"Odin?" Julie asked.

Jenn nodded. "I tried to explain to them what happened and that they should go easy on Luke."

"Really?" Julie was shocked.

"Do you remember what happened to Germany after World War I?"

Julie was taken aback. "I guess so," she said. "It was pretty terrible."

"It was awful," Jenn corrected, "and that is part of why the Nazis were able to come to power and eventually start World War II."

"Look who paid attention in history," Julie said.

"All the better to contradict the teacher," Jenn replied. "Anyway, that story the Norse have about the end of the world? That already happened. Loki did that because they were so harsh when they struck him down that he felt like he had to."

"So you didn't want them to do that again because then Loki would do something worse," Julie finished. She nodded. "Was that the only reason?"

They were here. Jenn put the car in park and looked at Julie. "I know you can read my mind," she said, "so why would you ask me that?"

Julie looked at her for a moment, but Jenn didn't let her in.

Julie nodded slowly and unbuckled her seatbelt. "Do you want me to tell them?" she asked.

"You'd probably better," Jenn replied, getting out of the car.

They had closed the front door, so Julie rang the doorbell instead of walking in. The girl who was missing a pinky answered the door. "Did you find them?" she asked.

"Yes," Julie replied, "but they couldn't come with us. Can we come in?"

Just then, two black shapes whizzed in through the open door and into the living room. The three girls raced in, to find that the two ravens had transformed back into their human shapes.

"You're back!" the girl yelled, hugging them immediately. Her other brothers came running down the stairs and began running Huginn and Muninn as well.

Jenn looked at Julie and jerked her head toward the door. Julie nodded. Neither of them wanted to intrude on this. They started edging out, when the girl saw them.

"Thank you," she said.

"It was nothing," Jenn said.

"No, it wasn't," one of the boys corrected her, stepping toward them. "I forgot all about being a raven, but I remember everything that happened now. Every day that we were stuck in that place, we just wanted to be human again and come home. And we did. When that man turned us back into ravens, I thought we were going to be stuck like that forever." He turned to Julie and grabbed her hands. "Thank you. So much."

"You're welcome," Julie replied. Julie was pretty when she blushed.

The boy looked down at their hands, and quickly let go.

"We thank you as well," either Huginn or Muninn said, turning to Jenn and Julie. "We have found a family on Midgard, and you have protected them, just as you have protected the world from Loki's treachery."

"You saved the world?" the girl asked, looking between Huginn and Muninn and Jenn and Julie.

"It's nothing," Jenn said desperately. "Don't worry about it." The girl ran over and hugged her. After a moment, Jenn hugged her back.

"Thank you," the girl said. "If you ever need anything, let us know."

Jenn was about to make a crack about needing the girl's other pinky, but she stopped herself just in time. "Thanks," she said instead. Then she pulled Julie out of there and almost dragged her back to the car.

"Not used to hearing praise?" Julie asked.

"Not exactly," Jenn replied, getting in her car.

"Then let me make you more uncomfortable," Julie said, closing her door. "You did very well. I know how unsure you were about what to do. You didn't know if you were going to go with Luke, or bash his head in. I know how difficult that choice was for you, but you made the right choice."

Jenn looked away and realized she was blushing.

Julie grabbed Jenn's hand and Jenn looked back at her. "You made the right choice anyway and you tricked the trickster."

Jenn laughed. "That'll be my new bio. 'I tricked the trickster'."

Julie laughed and shook her head. "You're really uncomfortable having a moment, aren't you?"

"A bit," Jenn admitted, starting her car.

"We'll have to work on that," Julie mused.

"Or not," Jenn said, driving away. "Hey. Do you have time to go get some ice cream with me?"

"Sure," Julie replied.

"Great. Let me take you to my favorite place."
**

The rest of the semester was so much easier without having to steal away to take magic lessons from Luke, although it was difficult to have to go through the bar and keep to their hours. One of the first things Jenn and Julie had to do was to turn off the traps Luke had talked about in his cave. Jenn did not want to find any more of those. Jenn and Julie worked on that particular wish for a long time. Eventually, they settled on, "I wish none of Luke's traps would hurt either one of us or anyone who means us no harm." After all, as Jenn pointed out, Luke probably had more enemies than the gods and some of them might not know Luke was no longer living in the caves. Or, if they did know, they might try to attack Jenn and Julie on principle. Secretly, Jenn thought it would be a great irony to use Luke's traps against him if he ever came around again.

One night, when Jenn was coming back to her dorm late, she accidentally used Luke's key to unlock her door. She opened it and was shocked to see the cave hallway stretching before her. Confused, Jenn shut the door and looked at her keys. Hesitantly, she put her dorm room key in the lock and tried that one. Now when she opened the door, it opened onto her room where her roommate was making out with her boyfriend.

"Can we get a little privacy?" the girl snapped. Jenn slammed the door shut.

Walking away, Jenn began to wonder why Luke had chosen the Velvet Tango Lounge as his base of operations but decided that the answer was probably that he genuinely liked the bar, or that he liked picking up women there. However, thinking about that reminded Jenn too much of the night she met him, so she dropped it.

Whenever Jenn had questions about her magic, she asked Abe, and she trusted his answers much more than she had trust Luke's. Jenn and Julie explained to Achi and Abe that Luke had been trying to change the world with violence. Jenn hadn't been sure if Abe and Achi knew, but they seemed to be surprised when Jenn told them and she had to believe that they weren't in on the plan and that they wouldn't betray Jenn or Julie. Julie had told Jenn they could trust Achi and Abe, so Jenn tried to content herself with that.

Julie still practiced her mindreading on Jenn, and Jenn got much better at keeping Julie out. Over time, they did turn the cave into a halfway house for magical creatures. Julie ran most of that, but Jenn was on hand to try to settle disputes, or trick creatures into trying out a better place to live. They agreed that when Jenn studied abroad in Spain over the spring semester and the following summer, she would keep an eye out for any creatures who might need a home.

Chuck, Helen, Emma, and Jenn ended up going back to the Velvet Tango Lounge again, but Jenn wasn't worried about it this time. She explained to her friends that she had told Luke to leave her alone and that he had listened.

"Then get me his number," Helen replied. "I'll take him!"

"I lost it," Jenn lied.

Then Emma turned the conversation to something else and Helen let it go.

Jenn, Helen, and Emma decided to move into an apartment together next year, although Jenn told them she couldn't find a place from Spain. "We'll just need thick walls so we don't hear Helen and her boys at night," Jenn said.

Helen pretended to be offended. "Jenn! I would only bring one home at a time." Then she laughed and shook her head. At first, Charles had pretended to be offended that they were leaving him out, but when Emma earnestly told him that her parents didn't want her living with a boy and that was the only reason, he relented.

"It's fine," he said. "I'm not sure I'd want to live with the three of you anyway. I'm far too manly for that."

"At least you're too manly for something," Jenn joked.

Soon enough, it was winter break and Jenn was getting ready to head to Spain. She and Julie both got an app so they could text internationally, and Jenn unlocked her phone so it would work in Spain as well. It was strange. Jenn was going to miss seeing Julie so often. She hadn't really felt that way about any of her friends before. "Maybe it's because we are actually friends," Jenn thought, shoving another pair of shoes into her suitcase. She liked having a friend. Maybe she would try to be nicer to her study abroad group in Spain.

It had occurred to Jenn that she was also using the halfway house to build an army of sorts. Still, it was possible Luke would remember everything one day, and she wanted to have an army at her back if she was going to go against a god. In the meantime, Jenn tried to figure out the rules of her magic and not to think about Luke too much.

Made in the USA
Lexington, KY
05 August 2019